Had he be~~en~~ ... there been the g~~listen of tears in~~ those eyes just a moment before?

Ricardo found himself wondering. A~~nd did~~ she know what it did to ~~him~~ ... ~~see the way that her~~ sharp white teeth had dug into ~~th~~e ~~pi~~nk softness of her ~~lo~~wer lip a~~s~~ she had look~~ed~~ down at their little boy?

He had lost any ability to read her expression, thrown off balance by what he had just learned. He had trusted her once, and that had had such shocking repercussions that he had vowed never to do so again. But this was very different. Vicious guilt clawed at him at the thought that his already hardened prejudice against her might have blinded him to the truth, driving him to misinterpret her behaviour after M~~...~~

He should wa~~...~~ ed, he resolved—in ~~...~~ more primitive resp~~...~~ even harder.

Dio santo, but he had had to fight with himself not to react on the most basic instinctive level. Every male impulse had urged him to reach out for her and pull her to him. To kiss away the imprint of her teeth in her flesh and soothe it with his tongue. He wanted to taste her again, know the soft sweetness of her mouth, explore the moist interior and kiss them both to the verge of oblivion.

Kate Walker was born in Nottinghamshire, but as she grew up in Yorkshire she has always felt that her roots are there. She met her husband at university, and originally worked as a children's librarian, but after the birth of her son she returned to her old childhood love of writing. When she's not working, she divides her time between her family, their three cats, and her interests of embroidery, antiques, film and theatre, and, of course, reading. You can visit Kate at www.kate-walker.com

Recent titles by the same author:

CORDERO'S FORCED BRIDE
BEDDED BY THE GREEK BILLIONAIRE
SPANISH BILLIONAIRE, INNOCENT WIFE
THE GREEK TYCOON'S UNWILLING WIFE
THE SICILIAN'S RED-HOT REVENGE
SICILIAN HUSBAND, BLACKMAILED BRIDE

KEPT FOR HER BABY

BY
KATE WALKER

MILLS & BOON®
Pure reading pleasure™

All the characters in this book have no existence outside the imagination
of the author, and have no relation whatsoever to anyone bearing the
same name or names. They are not even distantly inspired by any
individual known or unknown to the author, and all the incidents are
pure invention.

First published in Great Britain 2009
Harlequin Mills & Boon Limited,
Eton House, 18-24 Paradise Road, Richmond, Surrey TW9 1SR

© Kate Walker 2009

ISBN: 978 0 263 87430 3

Set in Times Roman 10½ on 12¾ pt
01-0909-52990

Printed and bound in Spain
by Litografia Rosés, S.A., Barcelona

KEPT FOR
HER BABY

For Anne and Gerry, to celebrate
this very special Caerleon Writers' Holiday.

CHAPTER ONE

THE heat of the day was fading from the atmosphere and the warm air was slowly beginning to cool. The shadows of evening had started to gather as Lucy carefully brought the small, scruffy rowing boat up to the beach where the edge of the tiny island sloped down to the lake and jumped out.

The cool shallow water swirled around her bare feet, coming up ankle deep, just below the rolled up cuffs of her blue cargo pants, as she tugged the small craft onto the shore, biting her lip as she heard the raw, scraping sound its hull made in the sand.

Would anyone hear that? She couldn't afford to be caught now, still too far away from the house to achieve her aim. If one of the small army of security guards that Ricardo employed had heard the noise and came to investigate then she was lost before she had even started. She would be escorted off the island, taken back on to the Italian mainland and dumped back into the tiny, shabby boarding house which was the only place she could afford to stay this week.

This vital, desperately important week.

If she managed stay in Italy at all. Once Ricardo knew she was back he was far more likely to decide that he wanted her out of the country as well. Out of Italy and out of his life for good. Just as he had believed that she was already.

'Oh, help.'

Realising that she was holding her breath, she let it go again on a raw, despondent sigh, pushing a hand through the tumbled blonde hair that had escaped from the band she had fastened it back with as her clouded blue eyes flicked rapidly, urgently from side to side, trying to see if she could spot anyone approaching. If someone had been alerted by the sound of the boat on the sand then surely they should be here by now?

It had to be safe to move. Dipping into the boat, she snatched up her canvas shoes, carrying them to the edge of the beach before she sank down onto the grass to dust off her feet and pull on the footwear.

She wished she could pull the rowing boat up further on the shore. Perhaps even cover it with leaves or branches so that it was more fully concealed from view. But she didn't have the strength to move it any further and the impatient, nervous thudding of her heart urged her to take other action, move on quickly.

Now that she was here, she really couldn't delay any more. She'd waited and planned for this so long, making careful preparations, and she couldn't do so any longer. From the moment that her letter to Ricardo had been returned to her unopened, she had known that this was her only way. She had to take matters into her own hands and do the only thing possible.

She'd tried the polite way, the civilised way and had been firmly rebuffed. She'd tried to appeal to Ricardo's better nature but it seemed that he didn't have one—at least not as far as she was concerned.

And so she'd been forced to come here like this, in secret. Like a thief in the night she had come back to the island in the gathering dusk, finding her way to the one spot where she knew that, tight as Ricardo's security was, it was just possible to sneak up close when hidden behind some bushes that overhung the lake. Paddling rather than rowing so as to be as silent as she could, she'd managed to get onto the shore without being spotted and now she could only hope that her luck would hold as she made her way to the house.

Pausing under the shady protection of a big cypress tree, Lucy found that she was blinking back bitter tears as she stared up at the huge neo-Gothic villa that rose up before her at the top of the lushly green sloping gardens. Carefully shaped terraces with ornate stone balustrades linked by flights of steps led up to the sprawling white-painted building that had once been a monastery and then later a palace.

The glass in the Gothic windows reflected the glow of the setting sun, and in the south western corner a tall tower rose, crowned by battlements sculpted in stone with floral decorations. From those windows in the Villa San Felice she knew you could look out across the calm blue waters of Lake Garda and see the provinces of Verona to the south-east, and Brescia to the west. Directly opposite was San Felice del Benaco, which gave both the island and the villa its name.

This amazing place, this fantastic house had once been her home.

But it was her home no longer. Not for many months now. And it hadn't ever *felt* like home in all the time she'd lived there…

Lucy shivered in spite of the mildness of the evening as memories assailed her. Distress made her skin prickle with cold goose bumps and she shuddered at the images that passed through her thoughts, reminding her of how it had once felt to be here. To live here and yet never feel that she belonged.

'I can't do this!' she muttered aloud to herself. 'I can't go through with it. Can't face…'

Abruptly she shook her head, fighting to drive away the unhappy thoughts. She had to face things, had to go through with it. Because inside that villa, as well as the terrible memories of some of the worst months of her life, there was also the one thing that mattered most to her in the world. The one thing that made her life now worth living.

Her feet followed the indistinct path with the ease of instinct built up in her time living on San Felice. She found the small gate into the private gardens in the same way, easing it open carefully and wincing in distress as the weathered wood creaked betrayingly.

'Please don't let anyone come,' she prayed under her breath as she dashed across the soft grass and into the concealment of the lush shrubbery that grew beside the lowest level of the stone paved terraces.

'Please don't let anyone see me.'

She had barely hidden herself again when she heard the sound of a door opening above her. The patio doors that led from the big sitting room, she recalled. The same doors through which she had made her escape not quite seven months before when she had fled this house, not daring to look back, terrified of what might happen if someone realised what she was planning and stopped her.

'Buona sera...'

The voice from inside the house floated down to her, making her heart stop dead in her chest so that she gasped in shock. A moment later it had kick-started into action again, setting her pulse racing.

Ricardo.

She recognised that voice instantly; would know it anywhere. Only one man possessed those dark, sultry tones or had that slightly husky note in every word he spoke.

How many times had she heard him speak her name in so many different ways? In amusement, in scorn, in anger. And yet, at other times—times she could no longer bear to remember—she had heard him speak to her in burning ardour, taking the simple ordinariness of her name and turning it into magic as he called her his *Lucia*, his delight, his passion...

...*His wife.*

Her heart flinched away from the memory of that word and the way that Ricardo Emiliani had once used it with a note of pride—or so she had thought at the time.

'My wife,' he had said as he took her hand to lead her away from the altar where the priest had just declared that they were married. *'Mia moglie.'*

And for a time she had gloried in the title. She had let herself enjoy being called Signora Emiliani. She had buried the doubts that assailed her deep under the cloak of happiness that shielded her from reality. She had smiled until her jaw ached and she had played the role of the happy young bride who had all that she could dream of.

When all the time, deep down inside, she had known the truth—the only reason why Ricardo had married her in the first place.

And love had had nothing to do with it.

'If you hear anything more, then let me know...'

The once-loved voice came again, startling her because it spoke in English and not his first language of Italian.

So who was he talking to in English? And why?

A nervous shiver ran down Lucy's spine as the sudden thought struck her that perhaps she might have made a fatal mistake in coming out of hiding and getting back in touch with Ricardo after so long. By writing to him, however desperate her need, she had let him know where she was. And Ricardo, being the hugely wealthy, hugely powerful man that he was, would have no difficulty in using that information to find out more. He had only to click his fingers and he had an army of men at his disposal—private detectives, investigators, ready to do anything needed to find out more, to track her down and…

And what?

What would the man who in one last dreadful row had declared to her face that marrying her had been the biggest mistake he had ever made in his life do once he found out where she was?

'I want to see this matter sorted out and finished with.'

'I'll get on to it right away. The contracts will be ready for you to sign tomorrow.'

Somehow it was the other man's voice that brought her back to reality with such a bump that she almost laughed out loud, only just catching herself in time before she gave herself away.

Who was she trying to kid? Why would Ricardo want anything to do with her? He had let her go without a second thought, hadn't he? No one had come after her to try and drag her back to this house and all she had left behind in it. And hadn't the message of the letter returned to her been loud and clear?

Contracts and signing—of course. What else would be on Ricardo's mind other than his huge luxury car business?

Ricardo Emiliani wanted nothing to do with her. He would never forgive her for what she had done, so now he was glad that she was out of his life and he wanted it to stay that way. She was a fool if she allowed herself even to dream that it could be anything else.

She shrank back into the shadowed space between the shrubs and the stone wall of the terrace as slow, heavy footsteps brought Ricardo down the last flight of steps and into the garden. Watching him stroll away from her, Lucy felt as if something or someone had suddenly punched her hard in the chest, driving all the breath from her body and making her heart jump painfully in her throat.

Even from behind like this, he still had such a potent physical impact that it made her freeze and just stare, unable to look away.

He had been walking away from her when she had first seen him. So the first impression she had had been of that proud, black-haired head, held so arrogantly high on a strong, deeply tanned neck. Her eyes had been drawn to those broad, straight shoulders, the powerful length of his back sweeping down to narrow hips and long, long legs. Then, as now, he had been wearing denim jeans so worn and tight that they had clung to his powerful thighs like a second skin. But that day on the beach, two years before, he had been wearing no shirt, nothing to conceal the bronzed skin of his torso, stretched tight across honed muscles that flexed and tightened with every movement, making her mouth dry in sensual response as she'd watched. He'd been barefoot too, seeming nothing but the casual holidaymaker she was herself, his appearance giving no sign of the wealthy, powerful man he really was.

She had been halfway in love with him before she had found out the truth.

Today he wore a white polo shirt, untucked at the waist and hanging loose. But she knew what was under that shirt. She had let her hands slide underneath his clothing so many times, stroking hungry fingers over the warm satin of his skin, feeling his shuddering tension as he responded to her provocative caress. She had closed her palms over the tight muscles of his shoulders, digging her nails into his flesh in yearning hunger as she had ridden his passion hard and hot until it had taken her right over the edge into ecstasy.

Oh, no, no, no, no, no! She must not think of that! She must not let herself remember how it had been, how she had once responded to him so fast, so easily. She couldn't let herself remember that or she would be finished before she started, her plan ruined before it even began.

She had come here for one reason only and that was…

A sudden sound, new and unexpected, broke into her thoughts, stopping them dead. For a moment it was as if it was so much an echo of what was in her thoughts that she almost imagined that she had conjured it up inside her head, wishing—dreaming—that she had heard it, rather than actually catching it in reality.

But then the sound came again, a snuffling, choking sort of wail, not too far away, faintly muffled, as if being held against something soft.

The world jolted beneath her feet, swung round once, and then back again the opposite way, leaving her feeling weak and queasy. One hand went out to grab at a nearby low branch, hanging on for dear life while her thoughts swirled and her head spun sickeningly.

'No…'

It was a low-voiced moan, one she had no hope at all of holding back. It couldn't be true. It couldn't be real. She had to have been imagining it, creating it in the hungry depths of her own thoughts.

But, as her clouded eyes cleared, she blinked hard and saw the way that Ricardo's arms were bent at the elbow, held in front of him as if he was carrying something, cradling it close to his chest. And as she registered the care and concentration he was exerting to hold his small burden, the way his down-bent gaze was directed at it, concentrating only on what he held, her heart clenched once again, skipping several beats in agonizing shock.

'Hush, *caro*…'

Once more that painfully familiar voice murmured huskily, the soft note in it tearing at her vulnerable heart.

'Time to sleep, *mio figlio*…'

Oh, dear God!

Mio figlio…

Somehow the new angle of Ricardo's body gave her a better view. Now she could see. And what she saw made her heart twist inside as if some cruel hand had just reached into her chest and wrenched it savagely, threatening to tear it right out of its assigned space.

Now she could see the way that Ricardo's arms were bent at the elbow, the way they curved around the small body he held. She could see the shock of soft hair—jet-black like that of the man who held him—that was cushioned in the crook of one arm, where the small head rested, relaxed and totally at ease.

And why not? The small boy was safe in his father's arms.

In a way that she once feared he would never be safe in his mother's.

'Oh, Marco…'

Her vision blurred, the harsh, bitter tears welling up at the back of her eyes, pushing against them until they ached and burned. An ache that was echoed deep inside her heart, tearing at her cruelly.

To her shock, she found that she had reached out a hand, stretching her arm towards the man who still stood with his back to her, oblivious to the fact that she was there.

No, not towards the man but towards the child he held. The reason why she was here at all. The one and only person for whom she would have braved Ricardo's anger, the fury of hatred she knew would be in his eyes when he saw her.

She had thought that she would never see her husband

again, and she had resigned herself to that. But what she had never managed to resign herself to was the fact that she would never again see the baby boy she adored with all her heart but hadn't been strong enough to love properly.

His baby boy—and hers.

Her son.

CHAPTER TWO

HER son was no more than a few metres away from her.

And never before had the phrase 'so near and yet so far' meant so much to her. Never before had it slashed at her with the cruel truth that she was so near to Marco that all she had to do was to take a couple of steps forward and she could be close to him. She could look down at him and see how much he had grown, how he had changed—because he had to have changed, surely, in the time she had been away.

Perhaps she could even reach out and take him in her own arms...

No!

Even in her dreams that was just a step too far.

She knew that Ricardo would never let her touch their son. And deep inside she really knew that it would be just too much to bear if she did. How could she reconnect with her little boy after all this time? She knew how the world would look at her—how Ricardo would see her. What loving mother, what good mother, would abandon her baby, walk out on him, leaving him alone with his father?

It had taken her long enough to accept that she had been ill. To acknowledge that she hadn't been able to find any alternative. The doctors said that she was well again now—but she didn't *know* it, deep in her heart.

Cruel, bitter tears flooded her eyes, blurring her vision. All she knew was that she couldn't stay in this hateful, appalling, 'so near and yet so far' situation and not give herself away.

She felt as if her already wounded heart would break, splintering into tiny pieces that scattered all over the paving stones at her feet. And yet this was what she had come this far for, after all. She had crept onto this island, sneaking past the security, just for this. The chance to see her little son.

But not like this. Not when she was not ready, not prepared.

And not with Ricardo Emiliani's cold, dark eyes watching her, cruelly assessing everything she did.

Stumbling slightly, she turned away. Not looking where she was going, not caring, she headed in the vague direction of the way she had come, hoping that she would reach the shore, and the boat, before the pain got too much and she sank to the ground and howled like an animal.

The crack that came when her foot landed on a fallen branch sounded appallingly loud in the stillness of the evening. There was no way that Ricardo could not have heard it. Freezing, Lucy tensed, waiting for the inevitable.

'Who's there?' Ricardo's voice was sharp, harsh in contrast to the soft tones of just moments before.

Not daring to look back to see if he had actually spotted her, Lucy plunged on, dashing into the bushes in the hope of hiding from his sharp-eyed gaze.

'Stop!'

There was no way she was going to respond to that…

'Marissa! Here—now…'

Behind her, Lucy vaguely heard the sound of swift footsteps—female footsteps—hurrying down the stone steps to where he was in the garden.

'Take Marco…'

That was the last thing she heard as she fled headlong, pushing aside branches that got in her way as she ran. Twigs snapped back, slapped her in the face, but she didn't care. All she could think of was getting away, reaching the boat and heading back across the lake. Anything other than facing an angry and aggressive Ricardo.

'Stop!'

How had he got to be so close behind her already? He had had to hand the baby over to Marissa—the nanny?—and then come after her but still it sounded as if he had made up so much ground that she could almost imagine that he would catch up with her at any moment. Heavy footsteps pounded behind her, making her heart race even faster in fear and apprehension.

'Giuseppe…Frederico…'

Ricardo was speaking to someone else. A swift, desperate glance over her shoulder revealed that he had taken out his mobile phone and had flipped it open, speaking into it as he ran, not breaking stride or even adjusting his breathing. A string of curt, sharp commands in Italian were flung into the receiver and Lucy's thudding heart lurched in even greater fear.

He was calling security. Summoning the trained body-guards who watched the island boundaries for him, protecting his privacy—and making sure that his baby son was safe. And now he was setting his bloodhounds on to her.

And he was not pleased. There was no mistaking that tone of voice. She'd heard it often enough when she and Ricardo had been together. That tone meant that security had failed him and he was furious. Ricardo Emiliani didn't countenance failure and heads would roll as a result of this.

A furious Ricardo was not someone she wanted to face. She had come here to try and talk to her husband, it was true, but she had planned to tackle him with the advantage of surprise on her side. Facing him now was quite a different matter. Seeing little Marco so unexpectedly had ripped away the flimsy protective shield she had built up around herself, taking with it several much needed layers of skin and leaving her raw and bleeding deep inside. She needed to get away, regroup and gather her strength again before she dared risk taking things any further.

The shore where she had left the boat was just around the corner. If she could just put on one last spurt, force her tiring and shaking legs into action, she might just do it. But whether she could get the boat onto the lake and actually get away was a very different matter.

Making a last effort, she pushed herself to breaking point, her breath coming in laboured gasps as a lack of fitness resulting from the past few months started to tell on her. She couldn't look where she was going, caught her toe on a clump of grass, missed her footing and fell headlong.

Or, rather, started to fall.

Just as she felt herself totally lose her balance, convinced that the ground was coming up to meet her, she felt a hand grab her flailing arm, clamping tight around her wrist and holding firm.

'Got you!'

With a jarring jolt she was jerked back from the fall, hauled upwards so that she balanced upright for just a moment, swaying precariously, before tumbling the other way. Straight into the arms of the man behind her.

'Oh, no!'

She hit him like a ton of bricks but, although he staggered

back, he didn't fall and the punishing grip around her arm didn't loosen for a moment. If anything, it tightened bruisingly so that she had no hope of pulling away.

'So who the devil are you?'

There was no way that Lucy could answer him. Her mouth seemed to have dried so much that her tongue couldn't form a word and her throat felt as if it had tied itself into knots.

But Ricardo didn't seem to need an answer. Instead, he adjusted his hold so that he could spin her round, bringing her to a position facing him where he could see her for himself.

'I said...*you*!'

It took every nerve in Lucy's body to force herself to look him in the face, though she flinched away from meeting his eyes, terrified of the darkness she would see there. She could almost feel the cold burn of his glare on her skin, flaying it from her bones.

'Me,' she managed and the uncomfortably jagged beat of her heart made her voice sound brittle and defiant.

The stunned silence that greeted her response stretched her nerves to near breaking point. In desperation, knowing he wasn't going to be the one to break it, she pushed herself to say something—anything—to try to show that he didn't totally have control of this situation.

'*Buona sera*, Ricardo.'

The sound of Ricardo's breath hissing in between his teeth told her that she'd caught him on the raw and the way his hand tightened about her arm betrayed the struggle he was having with himself to control the burning temper that she knew was flaring inside him.

But all he said was one word—

'Lucia...'

Her name. Or rather the Italianised form of it that only he

had ever used. The low, almost whispered syllables slid off
his tongue in a way that could have been a verbal caress or
then again might have been the hiss of an angry snake, pre-
paring to strike. And not knowing which brought her eyes up
in a rush to clash with his glittering black gaze, the ice in their
burning depths making her shiver in uncontrolled response.

'Lucia.'

He said it again and this time there was no doubting the
way that he meant it. The venom injected into the syllables
of her name made her quail inside, shrinking away from him
as far as his cruel grip on her arm would let her.

'What the hell are you doing here?'

Don't tell him the truth.

The warning words slid into her thoughts as if spoken aloud.

*Don't say a word about Marco. If you put that weapon into
his hands, then he will use it against you.*

'I said…'

'What do you think I'm doing?'

Somehow she found the strength to answer him, to put a
note of defiance into her tone. She even managed to lift her
chin in an expression of rebellion that was a million miles
from what she was actually feeling. And although she actually
made a pretence of looking into his eyes, of meeting their
savage glare head on, the truth was something so very different. Deliberately she let her gaze slip out of focus so that all
she could see was the dark blur of his face up above her. The
jet-black pools of his eyes were bleak hollows where no light,
no hint of feeling showed in their depths.

'I certainly haven't come to try to renew our marriage.'

'As if I'd think that was why you were here.'

Ricardo's tone was rough but laced with a deadly control
that refused to allow any real emotion into the words. And

although he still held her, she felt that his attention was not on what he was doing but on the thoughts that were inside his head. The thoughts that his icy command refused to let show in his face.

'Our marriage is over. It was over before it really started.'

From the moment he had accused her of trapping him into marriage. Of letting herself get pregnant purely to get her hands on some of the vast wealth he possessed.

'Well, that's something we both agree on, at least.'

Lucy tried an experimental tug to try to free her arm, recognising how much of a mistake the action was when Ricardo's grip tightened, restraining her without any real effort.

'If it's not that—*grazie a Dio*—then what is it?'

He was finally starting to recover from the shock of seeing her, Ricardo admitted privately to himself. Finally coming to terms with the fact that she was here, in front of him—the woman he had never wanted to see again for the rest of his life. The woman who had deceived him, played him like a fool. The woman he had thought was gone for good, out of his life for ever, and that had suited him to perfection.

And yet here she was, standing before him, her arm tensed against the pressure of his, her head flung back, her small chin raised, and those blue, blue eyes glaring into his in wide, determined defiance.

She hadn't changed much, he acknowledged unwillingly because he didn't want to notice anything about her. He didn't even want to look into her face, into that lying, devious face, and see the beauty that had once caught him, entrapped him—deceived him. A beauty that had once knocked him so off balance that he had forgotten all the careful rules by which he lived his life.

More than forgotten. He had ended up breaking every

single one of them and had turned his life into a form of hell
from which he had been only too glad to escape. The one and
only time he'd broken his self-imposed rule, he'd been caught
by a scheming gold-digger in the guise of an innocent lamb.
And he was not about to let that happen again.

She had lost weight, it seemed, losing some of the softness
of her face and her body. He wouldn't be human—or male—
if he didn't feel a pang of regret at the loss of the soft swell
of her breasts, the curve of her hips. But then she had been
pregnant for so much of the time they had been together that
naturally her figure had been more lush, the feminine parts of
her body more emphasised. If she hadn't been pregnant then
he would never have married her, would never have rushed
into the union that he had come to regret so badly. Would
never have tied himself to a woman he had come to detest so
savagely and so soon.

'If you'll let go of my arm, then maybe we can discuss this
like civilised human beings!'

'*Civilised!*' Ricardo scorned. 'That's not the word that
comes to mind when I think of how I'd like to be where you
are concerned.'

Now there was a word he would never use to describe
Lucy Mottram—Lucy Emiliani as she was now, though the
thought of his family name being attached to someone like
her brought a sour taste into his mouth. *Civilised* didn't
describe a woman who had deliberately let herself become
pregnant just to trap herself a rich husband, and then walked
out on her marriage when that baby had not even been two
months old.

'And it's not the way I'd want to describe your behaviour
in the past.'

Had she actually winced, flinching away in response to the

taunt? If she had then she had recovered almost instantly, tossing her hair back and glaring defiance up into his face.

'Equally, it's hardly *civilised* to hold me prisoner like this—just because you're stronger than me.'

'Oh, *si*—and if I let go then you will run off again and I'll never find out just what you're up to.'

'I'm not *up to* anything! And I promise I'll stay still.'

He'd be a fool to believe that. But, all the same, he eased his grip on her arm just a little. Out of the corner of his eye he saw that Giuseppe and Frederico, his damned inefficient security guards, had finally come up behind them, each one taking an approach from a different side, and he realised that he could at least afford to relax a little.

'I'd be a fool to trust you,' he declared, letting her hand drop in a gesture of deliberate distaste. 'But there's no way you can escape three of us.'

'Three bully boys onto one little woman!' Lucy flashed at him, her eyes sparking rebelliously. 'That's really balancing the odds.'

'There will be no bullying,' Ricardo tossed back. 'And you're hardly such a little woman!'

Deliberately he let his gaze slide over her tousled blonde head, her flushed face, and down the length of her body to where her narrow feet in the battered canvas shoes betrayed her mood in the way that they moved restlessly on the dusty path.

Her height had always been one of the things that he had liked most about being with her. The fact that he only had to bend his head just a little to meet her eye to eye had been a delight. The way that her mouth was just inches away from his when he did so had been a new and enjoyable experience after having to almost stoop in order to kiss the other women he had had relationships with.

Those eyes were what he remembered most about her in the past. The clear, bright blue that had seemed to reflect the colour of the sky on a summer's day when she smiled, or sparkled in amusement like the warm waters of the lake that surrounded this private island. At other times they had flashed in deliberate provocation when she had thrown a challenge at him. And then at other, very different times darkened into cloudy sensuality, heavy lids drooping into an almost sleepy look when all the time he knew that she had never been further from sleep. That her senses were on high alert, her body warming with awakening desire, her…

No!

With a brutal mental effort he caught his thoughts back from the dangerous path they were on. They threatened to scramble his ability to think, heating his blood and sending his brain into meltdown at just the memories.

That was the way she had caught him the first time around. That was never ever going to happen again. *Never*, damn it.

'So now…' his voice was rough with the effort of control '…I've waited long enough. I want an explanation and I want it fast.'

For a couple of seconds Lucy's mind hazed over as she struggled to find the words with which to answer him. Once again that warning voice sounded in her head and she acknowledged the fact that she couldn't let Ricardo see into the real depths of her heart. To do so would be to make herself too vulnerable, too exposed and defenceless. And she knew that, hating her as he did, Ricardo would take great delight in using her deepest need against her. He would exploit the overwhelming longing to see her baby again like a weapon and he could hurt her terribly that way, wrenching her heart into so many little pieces that it would be impossible to put it back together again.

'Lucia…'

Her name was a warning, a command and a threat all rolled into one and simply hearing it made her mouth dry in panic so that she had to swallow long and hard in order to find the strength to answer him.

'I…' she began, but he had already started to speak again, too impatient, too angry to wait for her to find the words.

'Just tell me why you are here and what you want!' he snapped. 'I've wasted too long on you when I have better things to do.'

'Better things like what?' Lucy challenged, stung by his dismissive tone. 'Signing more contracts? Making more millions? Or perhaps you have some hot babe waiting for you…'

The words shrivelled on her tongue as the image that they conjured up scorched her brain. She struggled to try to force away the memory of Ricardo in bed, as she had seen him so many times during their brief marriage, his jet-black hair ruffled and his bronzed skin dark against the whiteness of the sheets. She couldn't allow herself to remember how it had been. To do so would destroy what little was left of her self control and she knew that if Ricardo spotted just the slightest chink in her carefully protective armour then he would pounce.

But she had reacted too slowly. He'd already seen it and he had no hesitation in taking advantage of it.

'What's the matter, *cara*?' he drawled cynically. 'You're not jealous, surely?'

'What would I have to be jealous about?'

'What, indeed? After all, you were the one who declared that our marriage was over, and then walked out.'

Leaving your baby behind. He didn't actually say the words but he didn't have to. It was as if they hung there between them, big and dark and carved from ice.

And she knew that she was being a coward by avoiding them but she didn't dare bring the subject out into the open. Certainly not in front of the two muscular security men who were hovering just within hearing distance, obviously waiting for Ricardo to give a command so that they could take whatever action he demanded.

'And now you're back. And I'm wondering why.'

'Why not?'

Lucy aimed for bravado and missed it by a mile. She could only wince inside as she heard how sharp and brittle her voice sounded in the stillness of the evening, with just the faint lap of the lake water against the shore to break the almost total silence.

'After all, this was my home...'

No, blustering had been a mistake. She knew it immediately from the way that those brilliant black eyes narrowed sharply, always a danger sign in this man who had once been her husband. When his face changed like that, sensual mouth clamping tight shut, eyes seeming like gleaming slits above his carved cheekbones, then she knew he was at his most ruthless, his most coldly furious.

'*My* home,' Ricardo corrected coldly. 'A home that you only had a place in as my wife. A home you said you hated— a home you couldn't wait to turn your back on.'

The coldly obdurate way that he had said *my home* seemed to sear across her skin, burning away all trace of caution and pushing her into a total change of mood. He couldn't have made it plainer that she no longer had a place in his life, that he didn't want her here. She had only been tolerated because she'd been pregnant with his child, the heir to his fortune. Once she had given birth to Marco, all the tenuous value she had possessed had vanished. After that Marco had become an Emiliani and she...she had become nobody—not needed, not wanted.

Her fingers itched to slap that coldly ruthless look from his face but she knew that any such action would be a mistake—if only because of the still watchful, wary presence of the two security guards.

But there was more than one way to skin this particular cat and a wicked imp of inspiration told her exactly what to say to have the same effect verbally if not physically.

'Ah, but I've had a rethink since then and changed my mind. After all, I am still your wife, if only in name.'

'And only in name is all you'll ever be.'

'Fine.'

Lucy forced herself to give sort of a smile, knowing very well that it brought no light to her eyes and so made her look distant and disdainful.

'And as soon as I can arrange a divorce then I'll get rid of your name with relief. But there's one thing that came out of our marriage that I do want.'

'Of course…' Ricardo's arrogant gesture seemed to throw her words back at her in savage dismissal. 'I should have known that you'd come looking for the money you think you're entitled to.'

The fact that he thought she had come for money—and only for money—incensed Lucy, making her want to lash out, hurt as she was hurting. She was glad that she hadn't even mentioned Marco. Being the cold hearted man that he was, Ricardo was capable of flinging any request to see her son back in her face and walking away. But at least he had given her the opportunity to get in a few hits of her own before she revealed the truth.

'Not think, Ricardo—know. As your wife, then legally I'm entitled to a decent settlement.'

Could those dark eyes narrow any more? Half-closed though the lids might be, they still seemed to have the burn and force of a laser as they were directed at her face.

'Didn't you spend enough when you were here? As I recall, you damaged my bank balance pretty badly just before you left.'

The cruel words slashed like a blade, slicing into her heart, into her control and destroying every bit of command she had over it.

'I wasn't myself then! I was ill!'

To her shock and horror, Ricardo's reaction to her desperate admission was to throw his proud head back and laugh out loud. The sound echoed across the open space, seeming to swirl around the small bay and come back at them, dark, eerie and frighteningly cold.

'Of course you were ill.'

Hearing the sudden quietness of his voice, the complete ebbing away of even the dark humour, Lucy felt her head spin as if someone had just slapped her hard in the face, knocking her for six.

Was it possible that he believed her? That he actually understood?

'Oh, yes, you were ill, all right—you'd have to be sick to behave as you did. Sick to walk out and leave your baby behind.'

'It wasn't like that!'

She had to try to protest, even if she knew that he wasn't listening. The deliberate way that he had changed the words around so that he had exchanged the word 'sick' for 'ill', with its very different emphasis and meaning, told her all that she needed to know.

Ricardo's mind was totally closed against her. She could try to explain all she liked. She could offer any possible explanation to exonerate herself and he wasn't going to believe her. He wasn't going to listen and that was that.

But still she had to try.

'I can explain!'

But Ricardo shook his head in total rejection of the appeal in her voice, in her eyes.

'I don't want to hear it. There is no explanation that would justify such behaviour—none at all.'

'But Rico…'

Too late she realised the mistake she had made. In her fear and panic she had slipped into the shortened, softened form of his name that she had once been able to use. And the way that his face closed up told her that, if it was possible, he hated her for it even more than before.

'Please…'

But he was already turning away. She was dismissed from his thoughts, and his mind was already on something else as he turned to head back to where the lights inside the house gleamed out through the Gothic windows, emphasising the way that dusk had fallen as they had talked.

'I don't want to hear it,' was his callous declaration, followed by an imperious flick of his hand towards the two security guards, still standing as silent, stolid observers of the scene before them.

'Giuseppe…Frederico…escort Signora Emiliani off the island. Take her to wherever she is staying—and make sure she doesn't come back.'

He paused just long enough to let the words sink in before adding with extra emphasis, 'And this time make sure that you do the job properly. If she sets foot on this island ever again then you will both lose your jobs.'

Then he strode away, climbing up the slope towards the lights of the house without so much as a single glance back to make sure that his orders were carried out. He obviously had no doubt that they would be and that he could dismiss his soon-to-be ex-wife from his mind without a second thought.

CHAPTER THREE

LUCY was back.

Ricardo paced restlessly around the elegant white and gold sitting room, the glass of wine he had poured and then forgotten about still untouched in his hand. His thoughts were too preoccupied to allow him to drink, or even to let go of the glass his hand was clenched around, almost as if it was the arm of his errant wife, which he had held so tightly a short time before.

Lucy was back and in just a short space of time she had managed to throw his life into chaos just by reappearing in it.

'Dannazione!'

He slammed the glass down ferociously onto the nearby table, watching without a flicker of reaction as some of the ruby-coloured liquid slopped over the side and landed on the polished wood.

Lucy was back and he was damned if he knew what she wanted.

She had come looking for money, she had claimed.

Well, yes, of course she wanted money. What the hell else would bring her crawling back into his life when she had flounced out of it so carelessly and selfishly just over six months before?

She had to need money because she would be missing the more than generous allowance he had given her from the moment she had agreed to become his wife. The allowance that she had gone through with such speed and almost a compulsion in the weeks after Marco had been born. Then she had thrown money away on anything and everything that took her fancy, often buying half a dozen or more of the same item, in as many different colours as were available.

And then, more often than not, she'd discarded them when she'd grown tired of them, often without even wearing them, he recalled.

She must miss that allowance now that it was no longer hers. He'd cut off the supply of money as soon as he'd known that she'd left him—and the baby. At the time he'd foolishly thought that by cutting off her income he would bring her out of hiding more quickly, force her to come back to ask for more so that he could at least try to persuade her that her child needed her. But she had disappeared completely, vanished off the face of the earth, and even the extensive enquiries he had set in motion had been unable to track her down.

But she had to have lived somewhere and, with her bank account frozen, everything she had managed to stash away would soon have been used up so that she would have to come looking for more.

'No.'

Speaking the word out loud in the silence of the empty room, Ricardo shook his head as he moved over to the huge, high window that looked out across the lake and over towards San Felice del Benaco.

No, she wanted more than money. She had declared that she wanted a divorce, that she was putting in a claim for a 'decent settlement'. But, if that was what she wanted, why had she come creeping onto the island in secret, sneaking round to where he had been in the garden, watching him walking with Marco…

Marco!

Ricardo's hands clenched into such tight fists that if he had still held the wineglass it would have shattered in his grip.

Was Marco the real reason that Lucy had come back? Was she in fact here to try to get her hands on the baby son she had abandoned so heartlessly?

He'd die rather than let her! And no court in the country would give her custody after the way she had walked out on her child before he was even old enough to know her.

I can explain!

Lucy's voice sounded inside his head and in his thoughts he could see her face, pale in the gathering dusk, as she had turned to him. What explanation could justify her behaviour?

But what if there was some explanation—some justification that she could use against him? What if she had some story that she could take to court and try to claim custody of the baby—his son?

'*Dannazione*, no!'

That was never going to happen. He'd make sure of that.

There was one way he could ensure that his troublesome wife never got her hands on the baby she had abandoned so heartlessly. Lucy needed money and she would have as much as she wanted—more money than she could ever have imagined in her dreams…

…but at a price.

Snatching up the phone, Ricardo pressed a speed dial number and waited impatiently, long fingers tapping restlessly on the table top until someone answered.

'Giuseppe…' he snapped as soon as he heard the other

man's voice at the end of the line. 'My wife—Signora Emiliani…' His tongue curled in distaste as he made himself say the name. 'When you escorted her home, where exactly did you take her?'

Lucy couldn't sleep.

No, the truth was that she didn't want to sleep or even try to. If she so much as lay down on the bed and closed her eyes then images of the evening floated in her mind.

Images of Ricardo, tall and dark and devastating as ever.

Ricardo walking down the stone steps, along the grass. His long lean body silhouetted against the distant lake, his voice carrying to her on the still air of the evening.

And then that other sound, the faint, whimpering cry…

Marco.

Her baby.

Pain lanced through her, cold and cruel. A choking sob escaped her as she wrapped her arms around her body, feeling that she had to hold herself together or she would fall apart completely.

'Oh, Marco…'

The little boy's name was a moan of despair. Lucy moved to the small, high window and leaned against the wall, staring out across the darkened lake.

'So near and yet so far.'

Out there was her baby—her little son. Her arms felt empty and her heart ached with the longing to hold him. But if her visit to the island this evening had told her one thing it was that Ricardo was going to fight her every inch of the way.

You'd have to be sick to behave as you did. Sick to walk out and leave your baby behind.

Her husband's voice echoed in the bleakness of her

thoughts, black with cruel contempt. She would never get to see her baby again, not if he could help it. He clearly had no intention of ever forgiving her for what she had done.

And who could blame him?

Lucy swiped the back of her hand against her eye to wipe away the single tear that had welled up there, threatening to fall.

Why should Ricardo be able to forgive her when she couldn't forgive herself? She had walked out on her baby. But she hadn't known what she was doing. And she hadn't left him alone. He had had his father and the trained nanny to care for him. The nanny that Ricardo had insisted on from the moment she had given birth, making her feel useless and inadequate in a way that must have contributed to her breakdown. In her thoughts, they had been so much better for her darling son than a mother who didn't know her own mind well enough to know if she might be able to look after him—or if she would actually harm him.

She had hoped for a chance to tell Ricardo that. But he clearly wasn't prepared to listen. He had sent her letter back to her and now he had had her escorted from the island without a chance to explain. He would never give her another opportunity. She had known that he must hate her, but until today she had never truly realised just how much.

A sudden sharp rap at the door broke into her thoughts, making her start, her head coming up and her eyes widening in surprise. No one knew she was here.

'Who…?' Her voice croaked, broke on the word. 'Who's there?'

'Lucia…'

The husky male voice with its distinctive use of her name was too familiar, too disturbing. It was as if by thinking of Ricardo and their meeting earlier this evening she had conjured him up out of the air and brought him to her door. And that thought froze her in the middle of the room, unable to move forward, unable to think.

'Lucia!'

It was louder now, more impatient, definitely Ricardo. So definitely Ricardo that, in spite of herself, it brought a wry, remembering smile to Lucy's face as she recalled the times— the many times—that she had heard just that note in his voice.

'We can't have a conversation through the door. Everyone will hear us.'

Ricardo paused, obviously waiting, and in spite of the thickness of the wood between them Lucy felt that she could almost hear the irritated hiss of his breath in between clenched teeth as he waited for her answer.

'*Lucia!*'

Once again his knuckles rapped hard on the door. Clearly he had no intention of leaving. Suddenly afraid that he would take his annoyance out on the door even further, or that he would disturb other guests in the boarding house, Lucy was pushed into action, hurrying to the door and unlocking it. Yanking it open, she glared at Ricardo as he stood in the corridor.

'Are you determined to disturb everyone in the house?' she flung at him. 'Some of them may be sleeping.'

'Not at this time,' Ricardo dismissed with a swift glance at his watch.

'There might be children asleep!'

'And you care about that?'

'Of course I do!'

Too late she saw his face change and knew the direction of his thoughts. How could she care about other people's children, he was obviously implying, when she had walked out on her own son when he was barely a month and a half old? Didn't he know that nothing he did or said could make her feel any worse than she already did?

'I can't afford to cause any trouble that might get me thrown out of here. I have nowhere else to go.'

'So are you going to invite me in?'

'Do I have any choice?'

Not if she wanted to keep this private and quiet, Ricardo's burning glance said. And, knowing she had no other option, Lucy unwillingly stepped back, allowing Ricardo to stroll into her room. Those deep-set dark eyes subjected their surroundings to a swift, assessing scrutiny and his black brows drew together in a quick frown.

'*This* is where you're staying?'

'It's not so bad.'

It was pretty bad really, Lucy had to admit, suddenly seeing the room from his point of view. It was at least clean but it was definitely shabby, the flooring worn and the white covers dulled and thin from repeated washing.

'Hardly what you're used to.'

'Not what *you're* used to—or what you used to provide for me, you mean!' Lucy snapped back. 'I managed with worse before we met—how do you know what I've been used to while we've been apart? You stopped all my allowance, remember.'

Seeing the expression of dark satisfaction that crossed his face, she knew that she'd played right into his hands. He was thinking that the only reason she was here was because she was after his money. But then who could blame him? It was the impression she had set out to give in those few desperate moments on the island when she had been afraid to let him know her real reason for being there.

'There is such a thing as work—paid employment.'

Ricardo's scorn lashed at her like a cruel whip, the black contempt in his eyes seeming to flay her savagely.

'Or have you decided that that's beneath you?'

'Why would I want to work when I have a filthy rich husband?'

Determined to give as good as she got, she laid a bitter emphasis on the word *filthy*, knowing that she'd stung him when she saw his mouth tighten into a thin hard line as if clamping down on some more violent expression that he didn't want to let loose.

Just for a moment she feared—or was it hoped?—that he would actually turn on his heel and march away, walk out without another word. Instead, he pushed the door to with a bang, shutting them in the small room together.

A room that suddenly seemed so much smaller than ever before. Ricardo's tall, strong form seemed to fill the confined space, his dark colouring in stark contrast to the white-painted walls. She had not been alone with him for over six months— and being here, like this, in the intimate surroundings of a bedroom made Lucy's heart kick sharply, her pulse rate beating twice as fast.

In all her time apart from him she had never forgotten the sheer physical impact that Ricardo had on her. It was, after all, what had brought them together in the first place. That intense rush of burning awareness, the deep, hungry sexual attraction that had had her in Ricardo's arms within an hour of meeting him, in his bed just a few short days later. Just being with him had seemed to lift her life on to another plane entirely. One in which every sense was heightened, every experience felt new and wonderful. And the months they had been apart had done nothing at all to diminish the way he made her feel.

Every nerve seemed to prickle with excitement. She was so sharply, stingingly aware of the height and strength of him, the burn of those deep, dark eyes, the golden tone of his skin and the gleam of his jet-black hair. In the confines of the room she could even catch the clean, totally personal scent of his skin that coiled around her like the most seductive of perfumes.

Feeling overwhelmed and unsettled, she wanted to move somewhere—anywhere—to put a bit of space between them but the size of the room made that impossible. The only place to sit was on the edge of the narrow, uncomfortable bed, and just the thought of that made her stomach twist and knot so painfully that she pushed the idea aside in a second.

'I haven't been able to work,' she managed, keeping to the far side of the room while Ricardo paced restlessly around, making her think unnervingly of some big, sleek feline predator caged in a space that was too small for its size. 'Even if I'd wanted to.'

'No,' Ricardo conceded unexpectedly. 'You said you'd been ill.'

'You believed me?'

After his response earlier, on the island, she'd assumed that he would think the story of her illness was just that—a story—with no truth behind it at all.

The look Ricardo slanted at her from those dark eyes said that he wished he didn't have to believe her but he had no alternative.

'You've changed since I saw you—lost weight. But you're well now?'

'Oh, yes.'

That, at least, she could say without fear of how he would judge her. She wouldn't be here now, like this, if that wasn't true. Having forced herself away from Marco once in her life, there was no way she was going to risk having to make that terrible decision ever again by coming back too early.

'Yes, I'm fine.'

Fine didn't really describe it, would never describe it. Not until she had her beloved baby boy back in her arms and could make reality of the assurances that the hospital had given her. But, before that could ever happen, she had to deal with his father. And, because she didn't know why he was here, she didn't know how to handle Ricardo.

But he was here—and he had accepted that she had been ill. So would she be a gullible fool to allow herself to hope for something from that?

'I'm sorry,' she said, slipping into careful politeness in the hope of steering the situation into calmer waters so that they could at least talk civilly. 'I should offer you a drink…or something. But, as you can see, I'm afraid this room doesn't even boast a kettle.'

Her hand gesture, used to indicate the lack of facilities in the room, was a little too wild, a little too expansive. It gave away too much of the uncomfortable way she was feeling inside, the struggle she was having against the need to demand to know just what he wanted from her.

'I didn't come here for a drink.'

'No? So what did you…' Abruptly the courage to ask the most important question deserted her and she rushed on instead to a different distracting topic. 'I think I could do with one…'

There was a bottle of water and a glass on her bedside table across the other side of the room, just near to where Ricardo was standing. Without thinking, she moved to reach for it, stretching out her hand in the same moment that he did just the same. Their fingers clashed at the top of the bottle, tangling, pausing, snatched back, only to pause again, just touching, as they froze, barely inches apart, staring deep into each other's faces.

'Lucia…'

'Rico…'

Their voices clashed too, just for a second, then died away into stillness as silence reached out to enclose them, hold them.

It was as if they had both been struck by lightning. An electrical response had sizzled up her arm, fizzing along every nerve at just the feel of the heat of his body, the burn of his skin against hers.

Now she really did need that drink of water. Her throat was drying out completely in the wave of heat that seared her body, shrivelling her thoughts in its fire and setting alight the senses that she had barely kept under control from the moment that Ricardo had walked through the door.

'Rico…' she croaked again, unable to drag her eyes away from the burn of his glittering gaze, unable to move, unable to think, only able to feel.

And what she felt was the rush of awareness, of need that she had known from the first moment this man had touched her. A need and a hunger that had grown with each kiss, each caress. A hunger that she had convinced herself she could learn to live without as long as she was far away from him, never seeing him, never speaking to him, never touching him…

And she had managed it until now.

But she had only to touch him, have him touch her, and it had all sparked off again in the space of a single heartbeat. Nothing had vanished; it was all still there.

He felt it too. She could read it in his eyes, sense it in the change in his breathing, the way that a muscle jerked at his jaw line. It was still there, as strong, as sharp and as primitively intense as ever. Body speaking to body, sense to sense. Whatever had burned between them in the eleven months of their marriage, it was all still smouldering just below the surface, needing only a touch to make it flare into life all over again.

'Oh, Ricardo…'

Acting purely at the demand of her instincts, Lucy finally moved. Twisting her hand around, she let her fingers brush his palm, watching fascinated as his own fingers jerked just once, convulsively, as if about to close around her teasing touch, but then were abruptly forced still again. Those gleaming black eyes were suddenly hooded, hidden from her, concealing any trace of his thoughts. But Ricardo couldn't hide the way that his breath caught sharply in his throat, the deep swallow that struggled to ease the dry discomfort that matched her own.

Lucy let a small smile curl the corners of her mouth, grow until her lips curved upwards, wide and soft at the thought that at least in this one way she could still affect this hard, distant man as she had once been able to.

'It doesn't have to be like this. It really doesn't.'

'No?' Ricardo's voice was thick and rough, seeming to come from a throat that was so clogged with something raw that he could barely speak.

'No.'

Softly she let her fingertips drift over the palm of his hand, watching the strong hand quiver in uncontrolled response. Circling his thumb, she caressed her way over the powerful bones in his wrist, watching as the sinews tightened, the muscles clenched. It was impossible to control the need to touch him, impossible to fight back the urge to provoke him to react in a way that revealed that he was no more immune to her than she was to him.

To feel him close like this, scent his skin, feel the heat of him, made her mind respond as if she had slipped back to the days when she had been free to touch him, to caress him whenever she had wanted. She had loved those days, adored that freedom—adored him. And she wanted to go back there—wanted it, needed it so much…

'It never used to be this way.'

She didn't deliberately pitch her voice to sound so breathy, so husky. It just came out that way naturally. And right now she couldn't regret the way it revealed how the tiny physical contact had shaken her. How aware, how aroused it had made her. With her eyes fixed on Ricardo's taut face, she could see how, just for a moment, his tongue slid out to moisten suddenly dry lips.

Perhaps he too recalled the softer times in their relationship. The times before suspicion had changed him, darkening his opinion of her.

'It could still be…'

Moving her hand again, this time she curled it around Ricardo's, fingers lacing with his, palm pressing to palm, deepening the contact, making it more intimate.

And she knew her mistake as soon as she'd done it.

'*Inferno*—no!'

The harsh mutter was harder, more biting than if he had shouted. And the way that he froze, before deliberately, coldly uncoiling his hand from her gentle grip, pulling away almost in slow motion, was so obviously a deliberate insult that it stung like a slap in the face. With a flick of his wrist, he seemed to shake off even the last traces of her touch as he swung away from her, putting as much distance between them as it was possible to do in the small bedroom.

'It could not "still be" anything,' he declared, every word pure ice. 'There is nothing left between us, nothing I want to revive. Certainly not how it used to be. That is not what I came here for.'

'So what did you come here for?'

Determined not to show how his rejection of her had hurt, Lucy brought her head up defiantly, turning what she hoped were cold eyes on him as she injected every ounce of control possible into her voice.

'I take it it wasn't just to pass the time of day—renew an old…' she hesitated deliberately over the word '…friendship?'

'Hardly. We were never *friends*.'

'Husband and wife.'

'Legally, perhaps.' Ricardo dismissed her pointed comment with an indifferent shrug of his broad shoulders. 'But I doubt if we were ever married in the true sense of the word.'

'And just what, in your opinion, is the true sense of the word?'

'For better, for worse, to love and to cherish,' Ricardo quoted cynically, making her wince inside as the words stabbed at her.

'For richer for poorer…' she flung back, refusing to let herself think of the other words—the ones that said *in sickness and in health*.

If only she had been able to turn to Ricardo at a time when those words had meant so much, then how different things might have been. But she had known from the start that their marriage was never meant to be *as long as we both shall live*. If she had never become pregnant then he would never have married her at all. It was only because of his determination that his son would be legitimate that he had ever put a ring on her finger.

'For richer, certainly, in your case. You played your virginity like a trump card, withholding it from the poor Italian fisherman you first thought I was but only too keen to lose it to the rich man you then discovered me to be.'

'If that's the way you want to read it.'

It was the only way he'd ever read what had happened. He had never understood the very real fear that had held her back at their first meeting, forcing her away from him even though she'd feared she would never see him again. He would understand even less the bitter regret that had eaten at her for days afterwards, so that when she had met him again, in the very different circumstances of an elegant society party, she had been unable to hold back and, buoyed up on an unwise glass of champagne, had practically thrown herself into his arms.

'And I did not *play*…'

'You sure as hell did,' Ricardo tossed back at her. 'You played with both our lives—and the life of the baby we unwisely created between us. You told me…'

The temptation to put her hands over her face and hide from his anger—his justifiable anger—was almost overwhelming but Lucy forced herself to brave it out. She knew what she'd said. That she'd given him the idea that she was protected. But the truth was that she had been so wildly, blindly lost in sensation, in the heat and hunger that his kisses, his touch had aroused, that when he had muttered, 'Is this OK? Are you all right?' in a voice so thick and rough it betrayed only too clearly how close to losing control he was, she had only thought that he was considering her inexperience. She couldn't have said no if she'd tried. The only word in her head had been yes, the only need in her body, in her heart, had been to know the full reality of this man's sensual possession. And so, 'Yes, oh, yes!' had been her only possible response.

She had thought she *was* safe. The time of her cycle should have made her safe. But in that she had been stupid and naïve too.

'And richer is what you really want me to discuss. So OK,

let's get to the real point. You wanted to know why I came here. I came to ask you just one question.'

'And that is?'

'How much will it cost me to get rid of you?'

'Get…'

In the scrambled muddle of her thoughts, Lucy couldn't decide if it was shock, fury or just plain horror that kept her tongue from being able to form an answer to his question. She could only stare at him in disbelief, her eyes wide.

'It's a simple question, Lucia.' Ricardo's voice was tight with impatience and exasperation. 'Surely you can have no problem in understanding it. What I want to know is how much will you take to leave now, get out of here—and stay out of my life for good?'

CHAPTER FOUR

COMING here had been a mistake, Ricardo told himself furiously. A big mistake. A bad mistake.

And a mistake that he should have seen coming if he had any sense. Which he obviously didn't. At least not where Lucy was concerned.

But then sense had never been part of the way that he had reacted to this woman. His *senses*, yes.

Maledizione, he had always been at the mercy of his senses from the moment they had met. His mindless senses had rushed him into taking her to his bed, making her his—making her pregnant in the sort of stupid, irresponsible slip-up that he hadn't made even as a teenager.

It was those damn senses that had trapped him into a marriage that had been a mistake from start to finish.

And those same damn senses had been on red alert ever since he had walked into this room.

'How much will I take...?'

She was looking at him now as if he had suddenly sprouted horns and a tail. Those blue eyes were wide with what he would have described as shock if he hadn't known better. But of course he did know better. He knew just what his precious, greedy little wife was after, and all the pretence of shock and disbelief in the world wasn't going to make him think otherwise.

'You want to know how much it will cost you to have me leave?'

'That was the question.'

At least she had stopped the soft-voiced attempt at seductive persuasion. The *it doesn't have to be like this*…that she'd tried earlier.

She'd damn nearly had him with that. With the breathy note on the words that had made it sound as if she was totally overwhelmed at being here with him like this. Never before had he been so aware of the slender, curving shape of her in the clinging, worn jeans, the faded T-shirt. The scent of her body had seemed to surround him as he had looked down into the wide, wide eyes that had seemed almost hazy with need. And the soft touch of her hand on his skin…

Dio santo, but he had found it hard to resist that. That gentle touch had raised so many memories in his mind. Erotic memories that had had his body hardening in spite of his furious attempts to divert his thoughts onto other, less dangerous pathways. She had touched him like that on their first night together. Tentative, almost hesitant. As if she was shy and nervous.

Well, that shyness had pretty soon disappeared. It had evaporated like the mist over the lake at the first touch of the summer sun. In his arms she'd turned into a wild and seductive temptress. In his bed she had been the fulfilment of every sensual dream he could ever have imagined.

But they couldn't live out their lives in bed.

'So you're offering me a pay-off?'

'A settlement,' Ricardo amended. 'A generous settlement in return for a quick and quiet divorce—I'll even take the blame, provide you with grounds if you want it that way. And then you get out of my life for good. You go and you stay away. I never want to see you again.'

How could he ever want to see a woman who was capable of walking out on her own child, leaving behind just a frivolous, careless note that told him the marriage was over and the baby—Marco—was his responsibility now?

She was considering the proposition. Considering it seriously. That much was obvious from the way that her expression had changed, the softness vanishing from her eyes just before she let her pale eyelids drop down to cover them, concealing her thoughts from him.

'You really must want to be rid of me.' Her tone was flat, no emotion showing in it at all.

'Oh, I do,' he confirmed, his tone deep with harsh sincerity. 'Believe me, I do.'

'And you'd pay anything I asked?'

Her jaw had tightened so much that it drew in her cheeks, narrowing the whole look of her face and making the words come out as stiffly and as jerkily as if they had come from the carved wooden mouth of a painted marionette. Blue eyes lifted briefly to look into his face in a swift glance that was coolly assessing.

'In English law I'd be entitled to half your fortune. You should have thought about getting me to sign a pre-nup.'

If he'd had any sense then he would have done just that. But at the time the only thing that he'd been thinking of was the child they had created between them. The child that had to be born in wedlock and with his name as the father on the birth certificate. No child of his was ever going to grow up illegitimate, with all the snubs and the social exclusion that he had endured. The barriers to belonging that had blighted his mother's life as well as his own.

He had known that it was only his money that had convinced her to marry him in the end. But, if he was honest, then at that point he really hadn't cared. All that had mattered was getting the ring on Lucy's finger and ensuring that her name—and her child's—were the same as his.

He had thought that he would have longer to see if the relationship between the two of them would grow into something so much stronger than the wild, fiery passion that had brought them together in the first place and had resulted in the creation of the tiny life that Lucy had carried within her.

'And would you have signed one?'

At the time she would have done anything, Lucy acknowledged. Ricardo had only to ask and she would have said yes. She had been in so deep, so totally besotted so that she had been unable to think straight. She hadn't even hesitated over his proposal, though common sense should have told her that he didn't want her. All he had wanted was the child in her womb.

'I don't want marriage, Lucia,' he'd said. 'Never have. No woman has ever even made me think of it. But your news changes everything. We have a baby to consider and my child is not going to grow up illegitimate. That's all that matters to me right now.'

'It would have made sense—on your part, at least,' Lucy answered now, covering the lacerations on her heart with an armour of control. 'After all, neither of us was going into that marriage with any romantic stars in our eyes. We both knew it was just a business and legal arrangement.'

'And now?'

'Now? I wouldn't sign anything you asked me to without having it thoroughly checked out first.'

'Not even if it gave you everything you'd ever wanted—more than you ever dreamed of?'

'I don't think that's possible.'

If she could have Marco in her life, then she would feel as if she had been given the world and would want nothing more. But, without her son, there was no amount of money or possessions that could compensate for the emptiness his loss would leave in her life. And she knew, deep in her soul, that Ricardo would never let her have Marco.

'Try me.'

For the life of her, Lucy couldn't bring her numbed, bruised brain to recognise whether there was pure challenge or invitation in the two words that Ricardo tossed at her. And she didn't really dare to hope for the latter. Any invitation from Ricardo Emiliani came hung about with so many chains of doubt and risk, so many conditions, that it was like putting your head into a noose just to consider it. And a challenge was something she dreaded.

'Tell me what you really want—and you can have it. Anything, so long as you get out of my life and never come back.'

'You'll never give me what I want so there's no need to even ask.'

'Why not? I—' Ricardo broke off abruptly as a buzzing sound from his pocket drew his attention to his mobile phone. '*Momento…*'

Pulling it out, he checked the screen, frowning as he did so. 'I have to take this.'

With the phone clamped to his ear, he swung away again, listening hard and then firing sharp, incisive questions into the receiver in rapid-fire Italian that was too fast for Lucy's schoolgirl grasp of the language to allow her to keep up.

But she caught one word, clearly and distinctly, and that fastened onto her nerves, twisting and tugging with every second that passed.

'Marco…' he'd said. And, again, 'Marco…'

Whoever was at the other end of the phone had rung him because of something that was happening with Marco and just to think of that pressed Lucy's personal panic button, sending her thoughts into overdrive. Her heart was pounding, her breathing harsh and shallow. Something had happened to her little boy and she didn't know what.

She couldn't stand still, finding that only by pacing restlessly around the room could she keep herself from grabbing that phone from Ricardo and demanding to know what was happening. But the dimensions of the small space were restricted so that she found she had barely started before she was forced to turn and head back in the opposite direction. And still the conversation went on until she was ready to scream, only keeping a grip on herself by clenching her fists tight, digging her nails into the palms of her hands.

But then, at last, Ricardo thumbed off the phone and turned to her again.

'What's happened…?'

'My apologies…'

Their voices clashed, froze, then, because Lucy couldn't manage anything more, it was Ricardo who continued, his tone rough with impatience. 'I have to go. My son…'

Catching the look she gave him, he at least had the grace to pause in faint acknowledgement but only for a second. Immediately he continued, emphasising that possessive claim once again. 'My son has woken and is upset. I need to get back.'

'Is he all right?'

The concern wouldn't be held down. She didn't care what Ricardo thought of her, how he might interpret her enquiry. She only knew that if Marco was distressed then she had to know more.

'He will be when I can get to him.'

Once more the exclusion of her was deliberate, pointed. The words stung cruelly; as she was sure they were meant to.

'You left him in that big house—out there on the island—on his own…'

'Never on his own!' Ricardo cut in furiously and Lucy flinched from the fire that flared in his eyes. 'Of course he was well looked after. His nanny was with him.'

Of course, the nanny. How could she forget the nanny?

'He was asleep when I left…but he woke and she thought he was too upset to settle. She felt he needed his papa.'

His papa. Another vicious put down, slapping her in the face with the fact that he was Marco's father, the parent who cared for the little boy. While she was just an outsider. The woman who had given up her claim on her child when she had run out on him. For reasons she could explain if only she got the chance.

But now was not the time. Already Ricardo was turning towards the door.

'I have to get back to him.'

'Of course.'

But if she let him walk out of the door, let him walk away, would she ever get the chance to talk to him again? Would she ever even see his face again? And, much, much more important, how could she let him walk away when she knew that, back in the Villa San Felice, his baby son—*their* baby son—was awake and miserable and in need of comfort?

Not pausing to think, she snatched up the bag that was lying on the bed, stuffed her feet hastily into flat pumps and hurried after him. The speed and length of his strides had taken him out of the door and along the landing already and she had to push herself to follow him. She caught up just as Ricardo was about to let the main door swing to behind him.

'What the…?' The question was pushed from him as her hand clashed with his, catching the door before it slammed.

'I'm coming with you.'

'No way…'

'Yes.' She didn't know how she managed to get such strength into her voice. Determination perhaps, or just plain desperation.

What she would do if he refused point-blank to let her go with him, she didn't know. She could stamp her feet and demand that he let her—stand in the middle of the street and threaten to scream until he agreed. The problem was that, knowing Ricardo, he was more than capable of getting into his car and driving away, leaving her behind.

So she tried the opposite approach instead. She had nothing to lose, after all.

'Please,' she said. 'Please, Ricardo, let me come with you.'

And watched his head go back in shock, his eyes narrowing sharply as he studied her face.

Please…

Ricardo felt as if he'd had a knock to his head, jarring his brain so that he couldn't think straight.

Please. It was the last thing he had expected Lucy to say, at least in these circumstances and in that tone of voice. Correction, Lucy asking to go with him at all was the last thing that he had expected.

And she was *asking*. Making it sound as if it mattered to her. Making it sound as if she was actually concerned about Marco.

'Ricardo…' she said now, bringing his eyes to her face again.

In the light from the open door of the boarding house, she looked pale and drawn, forcing him to remember that she had said she'd been ill. What the hell had been wrong with her?

But he didn't have time to hang about here any longer. He

was needed back at the villa where, if the experience of the past few nights was anything to go by—and the sound of the nanny's voice on the phone had certainly seemed to indicate that it was—at this moment Marco was wide awake and roaring his head off in protest at the discomfort of having another tooth come through.

Oh, yes, Donna Lucia would just love that…

And that was the thought that made up his mind for him.

'OK,' he said abruptly, expecting and seeing the shock and blank confusion that crossed Lucy's face. 'You can come. Get in the car.'

A wave of his hand indicated the vehicle parked at the roadside.

'I…do you mean that?'

'Lucy—' his tone made his fierce impatience plain '—if you're coming with me, get in the car or I'll leave you behind.'

She moved then, hurrying to the car door and sliding into the seat as soon as he opened it for her.

Did she know what was ahead of her? Ricardo wondered. He doubted it. When Marco got into one of his crying jags then he made certain that the whole world knew that he wasn't happy. And, as far as his father could see, a baby boy in a bad mood didn't come with a volume control.

One thing was sure, if she hadn't already had enough of being a mother, as she had declared in the cold-blooded note she had left behind when she'd walked out, then the next couple of hours were going to push her as far as she could go. For even the least reluctant mother, Marco's screams could be positively the last straw.

And that was why he had finally agreed to let Lucy come back to the house with him.

If she needed any encouragement to persuade her to go, get

out of his life and stay out of it for good, then the sight and sound of his baby son in a tantrum was probably the most likely thing to provide it.

Which suited him perfectly, Ricardo told himself, slanting a swift glance at the woman beside him as she fastened her seat belt and sat back. A faint cynical smile curled the corners of his mouth as he started the engine, put the car into gear and set off down the road.

This was going to be interesting.

CHAPTER FIVE

THE noise hit Lucy's ears as soon as she stepped through the main door of the villa and into the huge tiled hallway from where the big marble staircase curved upwards towards the first floor. Even in a place the size of the Villa San Felice, the furious, distressed baby yells could be heard right through the house. And, hearing them, Lucy had a terrible fight with herself not to just forget everything that had happened, forget her ambiguous position in this house and run up the stairs as fast as she could, her arms outstretched to take her little son into them.

She had even moved part way to the foot of the staircase when Ricardo came past her, taking the steps two at a time, long legs covering the ground so fast that Lucy had to put on a burst of speed as she reached the wide landing in an attempt to catch up with him.

She only made it just in time as her husband pushed open the door to the nursery and strode inside.

'Marco...*mio figlio*...'

The soft words should have been drowned out by Marco's wails but somehow the quiet tones cut through his distress and had him pausing in the middle of his sobs to look up and see his father.

'Marco...' Ricardo said again, crooning the name, and im-

mediately the baby recognised his father. The wailing paused
and from his nanny's arms Marco held out his hands.

Reaching for *Ricardo*, Lucy suddenly understood, knowing
an appalling, terribly cruel sense of loss as she realised that
she had been about to step forward. Only to recognise, painfully and belatedly, that she didn't have the right to hold her
son. Not here, not now.

And besides—wasn't she fooling herself to imagine that
there might be any chance that Marco would recognise her?
She had been away from him for so long. And he had been
just a tiny infant when she had left.

She had to force herself to stand back, putting her hands
behind her on the wall as both a source of support and a way
of keeping herself from reaching out as she watched Ricardo
take on the responsibility of comforting their child.

Her heart was thudding violently, just as it had done from
the moment that the call had come through that Marco was
refusing to settle. Although Ricardo had made it plain that he
didn't think there was anything more seriously wrong with
Marco than a bad night and cutting some teeth, she had still
found herself imagining every possible worst thing that could
happen as the car had made its way down to the shore where
the boat was moored.

Luckily the speedy motorboat that Ricardo used to cross
the lake made the trip in a tenth of the time that it had taken
her earlier that evening in the heavy old-fashioned rowing boat
that was all she had been able to hire for herself. But, all the
same, the short journey had seemed endless as Lucy stood at
the prow of the boat, hands clenched tightly together,
watching the lights of the big house coming closer, willing it
to move faster—*faster*—so that she could be sure.

And now she was sure. Although miserable and irritable,

Marco was clearly not seriously unwell. But somehow, knowing that didn't make her feel any better. Seeing him safe in Ricardo's arms, the tones of a familiar voice reaching to him as his sobs eased, only made everything so much worse. She couldn't help but imagine how many other times this had happened, as the result of a banged knee or a miserable cold. How many times had Marco woken in need of a cuddle and she—his mother—hadn't been there? The doctors had said that she should forgive herself for that, but how could she forgive what she couldn't bear to think of?

'Calma, tesoro,' Ricardo soothed, pacing slowly up and down the room, the little boy in his arms. 'Calma...'

At last the wails stopped, the sobs subsiding to a low murmur and then a snuffling silence, broken occasionally by a faint hiccup, a slightly gasping breath. A small hand came out and patted Ricardo's cheek, gently, lovingly. Seeing the gesture, Lucy caught back a moan of longing and loss.

She would barely have recognised him. He was not the tiny, hairless little doll she had last seen but a small boy. So clearly his father's son, with the Emiliani jet-black hair and wide dark eyes. Eyes that stared up into his father's face with total confidence, total devotion.

Another shaft of pain ripped through her, tearing at her heart. She couldn't hold back a small choking sound as she struggled with her distress.

The noise brought the child's head round towards her. From the safety of his father's arms, his head pillowed on the man's strong shoulder, the little boy regarded her with wide-eyed curiosity, his soft brown gaze focused directly on her face.

'Oh, Marco...' It was just a whisper.

Did he recognise her? Was it possible? She longed to be

able to believe it, prayed he might show some sign—
however small…

But then those heavy eyelids drooped, his head lowered,
the small cheek, flushed with the effects of teething and his
crying jag, pressed against Ricardo's shirt. A small thumb was
pushed into his mouth and sucked on hard.

It was the last thing that Lucy saw with any clarity. The
tension that had been all that had been holding her upright
suddenly seemed to evaporate, leaving her whole body sag-
ging weakly. Her vision blurred as the stinging tears filmed
her eyes and all the fierce blinking in the world wouldn't clear
it for her. Her head was swimming, there was a buzzing sound
in her ears and she had to put a hand to the wall for support.

'Excuse me…'

She didn't know if Ricardo heard her, but the truth was that
she was past caring. If she stayed she would be a problem.
She had to get out of the room, get some air. She didn't dare
to look back at Marco for fear that seeing him would finish
her completely and she would collapse in an abject, miserable
heap right at Ricardo's feet.

She doubted if anyone saw her go.

At the far end of the corridor was a sliding glass door that
she remembered led to a balcony that looked out over the lake.
A place where on a fine day you could see the shore so clearly
that it almost seemed as if there was no lake. As if you could
simply step off the balcony and walk straight into the village
without getting your feet wet. It was all in darkness now, of
course, and as she leaned on the carved stone balustrade and
gulped in much-needed breaths of the cool evening air the
lights of the houses seemed to dance before her eyes.

The silence behind her told her that Marco was no longer
crying, that he had calmed, perhaps even now was falling asleep.

Falling asleep in Ricardo's arms.

A sobbing gasp escaped her as she wrapped her arms around her body, feeling the need to stop her heart from breaking apart. She had longed for this day, had dreamed of it for so many weeks. And yet, when it had happened, it had been almost more than she could bear.

She had so wanted to come back here, had so needed to see her baby. And yet now, when she was here, the only thing she could think was—did she really have the right to come back into her little boy's world? Did she have the right to stay, to disturb the routine he had obviously settled into with his father?

Ricardo was so good with him. She couldn't doubt the evidence of her eyes on that. It was so clear that this was not the first time he had comforted the baby through a disturbed night, soothed the little boy's distress when something hurt or he didn't feel well. Every movement, every touch, every caressing sound of his husky voice, carefully gentled to calm and reassure, made it clear that he had done this so many times before.

She didn't have a place here. She had given it up when she had fled from the villa, abandoning her baby. And wouldn't it be kinder, fairer…?

'So this is where you're hiding.'

Ricardo's voice came from behind her, making her jump. Clenching her hands tightly over the edge of the stone balcony, she tried to suppress the betraying start, only managing it by continuing to stare fixedly out across the bay rather than turning to respond.

'I'm not hiding! I just had to get out of the room.'

'Couldn't take it, hmm?' The cynicism in his voice had deepened. 'Who would have thought that such a small person could make so much noise? He has a strong pair of lungs.'

Lucy could only nod, not trusting her voice to say anything

about Marco. A mist seemed to have descended over the lake and it was only when she blinked her eyes firmly that she realised her vision was again blurred by the film of tears that she was determined not to let fall.

'Not quite your image of a pretty little baby lying sweetly in a crib?'

That brought Lucy swinging round, her eyes going to Ricardo's face as he stood in the opening of the door out onto the balcony. The unwise movement made her head spin sickeningly and it was a moment or two before she could focus properly. When she did, her heart lurched to see his dark and shuttered expression, the tightness in his jaw that drew his beautiful mouth into a thin, hard line.

'I knew he was not going to be totally quiet—you said he was unsettled. So I thought I'd better leave you to it. I'd have gone back to the boarding house but there isn't any way I can get a boat.'

'So you were running away again.' Ricardo's cynicism stung like a whip.

Moving suddenly, he strolled across the terrace to stand beside her, his back to the lake, lean hips propped against the stonework. Positioned like this, his face was in shadow and all she could see was the cold gleam of his eyes in the moonlight.

'I was not *running*…'

'Only because you could not find someone to take you over the lake.'

'I didn't know who to ask.'

'And it would not have done you any good if you'd tried.'

He leaned even more negligently against the wall and folded his arms across his chest. Lucy supposed that the position was meant to make him look more relaxed, totally at his ease. Instead, it had exactly the opposite impression. A shiver ran down her spine at the feeling that he was watching her intently, waiting for her to take a false step, make some mistake that she had no idea would actually be a mistake.

Or perhaps she had already made it and didn't even realise it. With Ricardo standing there in the darkness, looking like judge and jury all rolled into one, she had the terrible feeling that she had been tried and found guilty and she didn't know quite what she had done.

'No one would have taken you. My staff have been told not to take you anywhere. Not unless I give them specific instructions.'

Not just tried and found guilty, but tried, condemned—and *imprisoned*. The shiver at Lucy's spine turned into a full blown shudder and she grabbed at the balcony as her legs felt suddenly unsteady beneath her.

'Are you saying I can't leave?'

'That is exactly what I'm saying. Until I give permission for you to go, then you stay here.'

'I thought you wanted me out of your life.'

She might be worried—definitely on the verge of nervous—but she was damned if she was going to let it show. So she put the note of challenge back into her voice, lifted her chin as high as it would go and made herself meet the cold darkness of his eyes.

'After all, wasn't that the reason why you came to find me in the first place? "Tell me what you really want—and you can have it."' She quoted his own words back at him. '"Anything, so long as you get out of my life".'

'...and never come back,' Ricardo completed, making her wince inwardly at the sound of the words. 'Remember? That was the important bit. This time I want you gone—out of my life for good.'

He really must hate her, Lucy reflected miserably. And it was shockingly disturbing to find such revulsion directed at her, spiced with bitter venom.

'Hate you?' Ricardo echoed and, to her horror, she realised that she had actually spoken her thoughts out loud.

'Hate you?' he repeated. 'No, *cara*, not hate. I don't care enough about you to do that. But I do know a mistake when I see one and you—'

He unfolded his arms and one long finger came up, gesturing to indicate her slender form with a controlled savagery that made a nonsense of his denial of hatred.

'You are one of the biggest mistakes of my life. If not my absolute worst.'

The shaking in Lucy's legs was growing worse. Surreptitiously, she pressed her hand down harder on the rough stone of the balcony, needing the extra support to keep her upright. After a day of emotional shocks and changes, it seemed that her strength had been drained away, leaving her fuzzy-headed and unsteady on her feet.

'You know, that really doesn't make any sense,' she managed.

'No?' Ricardo scorned. 'And why not?'

'If I'm—' she had to drag in a gasping breath in order to give herself the strength to speak the hurtful words. '—the biggest mistake of your life. One you want out of here for good. Then why—*why*—are you keeping me a prisoner here?'

'Hardly a prisoner...'

'But you're making sure that I can't leave! Which amounts to the same thing. And why would you do that if you feel I was such a mistake in your life?'

It was the question he'd been asking himself all day long, Ricardo acknowledged privately. And the fact that she was asking it now too didn't make it any easier to answer.

He had never seen his relationship with Lucy as going anything beyond the hot, passionate nights they'd shared in his bed. But once he had found out she was pregnant then everything had changed. Their marriage had been for the baby and nothing more.

No, correction, their marriage had been for the baby and the hot blazing sex that had led them to create that baby. The hot, passionate sex that was the glue that had held them together in the place of anything else. And that he had thought would hold them together until they could put something else in its place.

Because, OK, they had rushed into marriage purely for convenience and to ensure that Marco was legitimate. But surely, when the baby was born, they could have taken some time to get to know each other properly. To find out if there was anything more than that blazing passion that had yoked them together from the start.

But Lucy hadn't stayed around long enough to find out if that was the case. No sooner had Marco been safely delivered than she had launched herself into a lifestyle from which he—and the baby—were totally excluded. She had been out on the town every day, spending money like water, bringing home innumerable carrier bags of clothes, shoes, make-up. Most of which she had never worn or used. She had moved into a separate room, had had to be cajoled into seeing her son, was blatantly reluctant to care for him, leaving him instead to the care of his nanny almost twenty-four hours a day.

Then, within six weeks, she had simply walked out. Leaving a heartless note that made it plain just what she had wanted out of the marriage. It hadn't been Marco—and it most definitely hadn't been a life with Ricardo. All she had wanted was the lifestyle, the luxury, that his wealth had brought.

I gave you the son you wanted and almost a year of my life. Think that's quite long enough. You can have Marco—after all, he's the only reason we went through this farce of a marriage—and I'll have my freedom. I'll be in touch about the divorce.

And now here she was. Just as she had promised. She had come back into his life for the sole purpose of doing just that—talking about the divorce. And, of course, just how much she was going to get in her settlement.

He detested her. He hated who she was, what she'd done. So why in the devil's name would he try to keep her with him any longer than he had to?

'We haven't talked about the divorce. About what you want out of it.'

Had he actually touched a nerve there? Was it possible that she could be affected by what he had said? Certainly it looked as if some sort of a light—the light of challenge and defiance had gone out of her eyes. Or was it merely some trick of the moon that had taken that from her gaze in the same way that it seemed to have drained the colour from her face?

'When we have an agreement, then you can go. I'll have Enzo bring the launch around and you can be back on the shore in less than fifteen minutes. I'll even give you an advance on your settlement so that you can book yourself into a decent hotel—providing you get the first plane from Verona Airport tomorrow morning.'

Once again it seemed that he had caught her on the raw. She actually flinched, wincing away from his words. A frown creased the space between his brows but, just as he was leaning forward in some concern, her head came back up again, blue eyes flashing defiance.

'No!'

Just for a moment she looked almost as if the force of her refusal had taken her by surprise as much as him. Those clear, bright eyes seemed to go out of focus for a second, then came back to clarity again as she blinked hard. She swayed suddenly as if buffeted by an unexpectedly strong wind that had blown up out of nowhere but then straightened again, fixing her furious gaze on his face once more.

'That isn't going to happen! I won't go!'

'Won't?'

Ricardo frowned his deep confusion, trying to read just what sort of mood she was in.

'Now you're the one who's not making sense. A moment ago you couldn't wait to get away.'

'Yes…but…I can't go like this.'

'Yes. you can. It's quite simple—all you have to do is to tell me what you want and I'll give…'

'But you won't!' Lucy cut in, her voice sharp and shaking, her hands coming up in a wild gesture to emphasise her words. 'You won't give it to me.'

'I gave my word.'

She was shaking her head violently, sending her hair flying out around her in a crazily flurried halo.

'But you won't keep it!'

'I will—damn it, Lucia—I promise…'

'Don't promise what you can't…won't…'

It was as she shook her head again, clearly on the edge of losing things completely, that Ricardo felt his own control crack. That swirling hair had brushed against his face, the feel, the scent of it bringing so many memories rushing to the surface of his mind.

How could he ever forget the fresh, clean scent of it,

perfumed by some herbal shampoo that tantalised his senses?
Or how it had felt to know the silken slither of that long
blonde hair over his skin as she knelt above him, his body
sheathed in hers? As his groin tightened in instant response
he almost felt again the slow, sensual movements that had
driven him to the edge of his control, keeping him there in
subtle torture until he could take no more.

'Lucia—stop...' he growled, reaching for her flailing
hands. 'Stop it, now! This isn't doing you any good.'

The rough little shake was just meant to force her to
rethink, to come back to herself. But when she threw back her
head, drawing in a ragged breath, ready to speak again, he
knew that touching her had been a mistake. A big mistake.

A mistake he had been heading towards all evening. Ever
since that moment when she had touched his arm earlier in
the shabby little room in the boarding house. No—earlier
than that, when she had been about to fall and he had caught
her, yanking her upright so that she had slammed hard against
him. Her body pulled into close and intimate contact with his.

Just recalling that made his heart kick up a pace, his breath
coming raw and uneven into his lungs. His hands tightened
even more about her arms, moving upwards, towards her
shoulder, stilling her, holding her...

And, in that moment, she looked up into his face, her soft
pink mouth half open, her breath coming as unevenly as his.
Their eyes caught and clashed, held and...

And all control left him as he saw her eyes widen, saw the
shocked response and then the sensual awareness that clouded
them. It clouded his mind too, leaving him no ability to think.
He could only feel.

And hunger.

And that hunger drove him into mindless action, pushing

him into hauling her hard up against him, wrenching her chin up towards him and clamping his mouth down hard on hers. Letting loose a rough grunt of satisfaction as he felt her lips give, opening instinctively under the hard, fierce pressure of his kiss.

A small murmur of distress got through to him, ripping apart the clouds of burning sensuality that clouded his mind, bringing a flash of rational clarity to his heated brain. Immediately he gentled his kiss, easing the pressure on her mouth, using softness, enticement, seduction to counter the brute force he had subjected her to just moments before.

It started out hard to silence her, control her. He had snatched at her lips, trying to crush back the cries of distress, stop them from pouring from her mouth. He didn't understand why she should be so upset, why she was in such a state, but there would be no talking to her until she had calmed down.

'Hush, Lucia, hush… There's no need for this. Whatever you need—whatever you want—whatever trouble you've got yourself into—I'll deal with it.'

That stopped her, froze her. She could only stare mutely into his face, her expression white and strained, huge eyes colourless in the moonlight. With a devastating sense of shock, Ricardo realised that the strange glitter on their surface was not the effect of the pale, cold moonlight but the glisten of unshed tears.

'Lucia?' It was a shocked whisper. And his next kiss was soft, gentle, wanting to wipe the upset from her lips. He took her mouth slowly, carefully, and his heart seemed to stop dead, then start up again in double-quick time, ragged and uneven as he felt the tiny, involuntary, almost automatic softening of her lips in response, the gentle pressure of her mouth against his.

The scent of her skin was all around him. The slide of her hair was against his hands. The softness of her body was in his arms, tight against him. And deep inside the hunger was waking, starting to grow.

But, even as he slid his hands down her back, he knew that something had changed. Lucy had hesitated, drawn back faintly, then a little more strongly, putting her hands on his chest to push him away from her.

'You mustn't do this. You shouldn't.'

'Why not?' Trying to make light of it, he even tried a rough laugh deep down in his throat. 'You were becoming hysterical. Something had to be done—and there are only two traditional ways to calm a hysterical woman. You surely wouldn't have wanted me to slap you.'

Numbly she shook her head, her eyes glazed with something that looked close to despair. 'You might wish you'd done that when I tell you.'

'When you tell me what? Damnation, Lucia, what the hell are you talking about? What is it that you want? And why are you so sure that I won't give it to you?'

Her hesitation caught him on the raw, tugging on nerves that suddenly felt painfully exposed, desperately vulnerable. A terrible sense of oppression shot through him, a prediction of something that was coming that he wasn't going to like at all.

'Because you won't give me Marco. And that's what… who I want…nothing else. The only thing in the world that I want is my son.'

If she had spat right in his face he couldn't have been more appalled. As it was, he felt the sense of dark shock reverberate through him so that he released her at once, almost dropping her to the ground as if she had turned into a poisonous snake in his arms. From wanting to hold her so close, he jumped to the sense that holding her would contaminate him in the space of a single devastated heartbeat.

'Marco? You came here for *Marco*? To take him…'

Unable to find the words, Lucy just nodded, then immediately realised that that was just what she should not have done. She hadn't come to *take* Marco, not in the way that Ricardo meant. But it was already too late. She had nodded and she watched Ricardo's face close down, the tightness of his jaw and the darkness in his eyes making her shiver.

'Never,' he said and the word was disgust, an ultimatum, a warning and a threat all rolled into one. 'After what you did? Not in my lifetime.'

'But—' Lucy's voice broke on the word. 'I can explain…'

'You can try. But I cannot imagine that anything you say will ever convince me.'

He paused, waited, head slightly tilted to one side, giving her such a pointed look that she practically felt it scrape over her skin like the sharp end of a needle, raising a raw, red weal.

He would listen, that look said, but he would not believe. He was already armoured against her. Even if she mentally beat her fists hard against his unyielding defences until they were raw and bleeding, he would not let her reach him.

'So…' he goaded when she still didn't speak, couldn't find a way to start '…explain.'

She wished she could. But how could she say anything when those cold black eyes seemed to probe her skull as her brain frantically tried different ways of beginning and discarded each one as unusable? At least that was what she thought she was doing but her thoughts seemed so completely unfocused that she found that nothing she tried made sense. And nothing would form clearly so that she could follow it through for herself, let alone explain it to Ricardo so that he would understand and believe her.

Because he had to believe her.

'You can't, can you? Because there isn't an explanation.
Not one that would satisfy anyone else. And certainly not
someone who loves Marco.'

'*I* love him…'

Her voice sounded frail, just a thin thread of sound—what
she could hear of it over the buzzing inside her skull. It was
as if a swarm of bees had suddenly invaded her head and were
swirling round and round inside it.

'Love him!' Ricardo scorned 'How can you say that? How
dare you say that? You left him! Abandoned him…'

'I know and that was wrong—but I was ill. I'm back now.
And I want…'

'You want?' Ricardo echoed, his voice a vicious snarl.
'You *want*—always what you want! Well, let me tell you,
cara, that what you want is not going to happen—never. Not
while I live. Not while I can stop you. And if "I love him" is
the best damn explanation that you can come up with then, to
be honest, lady, I don't want to hear it.'

He was turning away as he spoke, using his body as well
as his face, which was set hard and cold against her, to express
the way he felt.

'Ricardo, please…'

She had to stop him; had to make him listen. Lurching
forward, she tried to grab at his arm, to hold him back, but
missed. Her hand, aiming for the hard strength of his arm,
found instead only empty air and waved wildly, frantically.
The awkward movement threw her right off balance, jarring
her head nastily.

The buzzing in her head grew louder, wilder and a burning
haze seemed to rise before her eyes, blinding her completely.

'Ricardo!' she cried on a very different note as the world
swung round her, lurching violently. Her hand groped for

support, found it for a moment in the feel of muscle under warm, hair-hazed skin.

Then she lost it again as her grip loosened completely. A wave of darkness broke over her and she slid to the ground in a total faint.

CHAPTER SIX

'ARE you awake?'

The voice, huskily male and disturbingly familiar, broke through the clouds of sleep that filled Lucy's head, making her stir in the bed, frowning slightly as her head moved on the pillows.

Softer pillows than she remembered. She must have got used to the conditions in the boarding house. The first night they had felt so rough and lumpy, but now…

'Lucy! It is time to wake up.'

The voice came again, rough and impatient now. It broke into the wonderful oblivion of much needed sleep that had hidden everything from her, almost wiping her memory clear of all that had happened.

Until the sound of Ricardo's voice brought it all back in a way that had her bolting upright in the bed, staring wide-eyed at the figure standing in the middle of the room.

'What has happened? Where am I?'

'*Buon giorno, bella* Lucia,' Ricardo drawled lazily, strolling across the room to lounge at the end of the bed.

Propping one hip against the ornately carved wooden bed frame, he pushed his hands deep into the pockets of the jeans he wore with a deep red polo shirt, open at the throat.

'You have no need to panic; you are quite safe. You are in the Villa San Felice, just as you were last night. So one might say that in fact you have come home.'

'*Home* is not a word I associate with this place!' Lucy tossed at him as she tried to collect her scrambled thoughts, feeling that panicking was exactly what she *should* be doing. 'Nowhere where you are could ever be home to me.'

She was more aware of her surroundings now. Aware enough to recognise and be thankful for the fact that at least this was just one of the smaller bedrooms in the east wing of the villa. To her intense relief, the heavy wooden furniture and the soft blue curtains and carpet were not the ones she remembered from the room she had shared with Ricardo in her time as his wife. She didn't feel that she would have been able to hold herself together if she had woken to find herself in their suite.

'So how did I get here? What happened?'

Ricardo pushed a long hand through the darkness of his hair, disturbing its sleek black strands and his piercing eyes never left her flushed face as he observed every change of expression, every fleeting emotion that crossed it.

'You were taken ill—you passed out. Do you not recall?'

'No…I…'

But then she did remember everything in a rush. From the moment she had set out on her attempt to get onto the island, to see Marco…

Marco…

'I fainted,' she managed, piecing the events back together in her thoughts. 'And you…'

The memory of Ricardo's voice, his cruel words, swirled inside her head, making her feel dizzy just from the thought of it.

You are one of the biggest mistakes of my life. If not my absolute worst.

'How did I get to be here? Who brought me…'

'I brought you here,' Ricardo inserted calmly, the smooth tones of his voice sliding into the rising hysteria of hers. 'And yes—before you ask, I put you to bed.'

'You…'

If he had slapped her across the face he couldn't have brought her up sharp any more forcefully than that. Suddenly she became aware of the fact that she was sitting upright against the pillows with the soft comfort of the downy quilt slipping down to fall around her waist, exposing the top half of her body.

The top half of her body that was now wearing only the thin, plain bra that cupped her breasts.

'You undressed me!'

Hot blood rushed into her cheeks, then ebbed away again almost at once as she snatched at the coverings, yanking them up to her neck to conceal herself, protect her body from those probing eyes. But just too late to erase the sensation of his searching gaze raking over her skin, flaying off a much-needed protective layer. It was impossible not to remember how he had once used to undress her—undress her so softly, so gently, or at other times almost ripping the clothes from her with such a wild urgency that her heart threatened to burst with just the memory of it.

'I undressed you,' Ricardo confirmed.

His beautiful mouth twitched, just once, in an expression that could have been anything—amusement, annoyance, contempt or just plain triumph. Lucy had no idea which, and the hot embarrassment that was flooding her thoughts left her incapable of even trying.

'And why should that disturb you? Surely it was better…'

'Better!' Lucy interrupted, still struggling with the uncomfortable feeling of being…violated was the only word that came to mind. She knew that Ricardo would dismiss it as being exaggerated and overblown, and deep down she knew that it was. But it was how she felt all the same at just the thought of those long tanned hands unbuttoning her shirt, sliding it from her, taking her jeans…

'And tell me just why it's better to have you manhandle me…'

'I did not manhandle you!'

She'd caught him on the raw there, sending sparks into the darkness of his eyes and making him bite out the words in a tone of barely controlled fury that had her flinching back against the pillows and pulling the duvet even more tightly around her in spite of the warmth of the sun that was coming in through the narrow arched window. Beyond that window she could hear the calm blue waters of the lake lapping lazily against the stony shore and then ebbing back again with a faint sucking sound as they pulled against the tiny pebbles. It seemed unnaturally loud in the dangerous silence that descended before Ricardo drew in a long harsh breath.

'I have never 'manhandled' a woman in my life and I do not intend to start with my wife. Because surely that is the point here—that I—as your husband—performed this duty for you myself rather than leave it to a stranger.'

'You are not my husband!'

Lucy wouldn't have believed that it was possible for Ricardo's expression to grow any more glacial or for the cold anger in his eyes to burn any more savagely but clearly her words had provoked him into darker fury as he flung a glance of bitter recrimination in her direction.

'We took the vows,' he declared icily. 'We were married.'

'But only to make sure that our son was born legitimate with two married parents to be named on his birth certificate. Beyond that, the whole thing meant nothing—and the vows less than nothing. I didn't want to marry you and you…'

'I wanted you as my wife.'

'Because I was Marco's mother. Oh, come on, Ricardo, are you telling me that if I hadn't got pregnant you would still have asked me to marry you?'

'No…'

'No.' She tried to make it sound as if his answer satisfied her, but the truth was that there was no satisfaction to be found in the single word. 'I thought not.'

'I wanted you…'

'Oh, I know…' She couldn't keep the bleakness, the bitterness from her voice. 'You made that only too plain. But you could have had me in your bed without tying yourself— without tying both of us—down to marriage. But I got pregnant and that trapped us, Ricardo. Trapped us in a marriage that neither of us wanted.'

It was weak, it was foolish—it was downright masochistic—but all the same she couldn't stop herself from pausing, waiting just a second, just long enough for her stupidly vulnerable heart to give a couple of unsteady, jerky beats just in case Ricardo actually thought about *denying* that statement.

Well, if she'd hoped it might happen then she was destined for disappointment. He remained stubbornly silent, forcing her to go on.

'And now I want to get out of it. We both want to get out of it. Which is why it's not…appropriate…for you to…'

'For me to do what?' Ricardo cut in, satire burning in the words. 'Not appropriate for me to help a woman who is evidently unwell and who has fainted at my feet? Not appropriate to pick her up and carry her inside, put her into a comfortable bed—and perhaps remove her outer clothing so that she may sleep more comfortably? I think that only you would assign some sort of sexual motive to that.'

His cynicism lashed at her, making her flinch inwardly. Her face was burning once more but this time with a very different sort of embarrassment. Hearing it like that, it did sound so perfectly innocent. Did she really think that she was so sexually irresistible that he was unable to keep his hands off her?

If she had been foolish enough to even consider any such thought then his tone and the blazing fury in his eyes would have very soon disillusioned her. Ricardo might have once been so determined and so hungry to get her into his bed that he had broken what he had told her was normally an indestructible rule and made love to her without using a condom, but it clearly was not the case any more. He had seen her as nothing more than some woman who needed help and he had acted accordingly.

'You did that?' Her whole body was burning with embarrassment so that the words quavered on her tongue. 'Thank you—and I'm sorry.'

A swift, curt nod was Ricardo's only acknowledgement of her response and almost immediately it seemed that his mind had moved on to something else.

'Someone had to take care of you. You obviously weren't taking care of yourself. Tell me, Lucia—when did you last eat?'

The question was unexpected, catching her off guard and forcing her to consider.

'Yesterday…' she said slowly, still thinking about it.

'Are you sure?'

No, she wasn't sure. Yesterday morning she had known that she was going to try to get onto the island. That she was going to try to see Marco. And that had left her nerves so tightly strung that her stomach had clenched painfully from the moment that she had woken up, and it had stayed like that all day. And the day before...

'You told me that you had been ill.'

She'd told him but, if he was honest, he hadn't considered that it was serious, Ricardo admitted to himself. But when she had collapsed at his feet then he had had to take notice. And picking her up to carry her indoors had sent a sensation like a brutal kick straight to his guts.

She had lost so much more weight than he had realised. In his arms she had felt as fragile and vulnerable as a lost bird, one that had fallen from the nest before it had quite learned how to fly. Beneath the protection of her clothing, she was skin and bone, and the way that stabbed at his conscience was uncomfortable and disturbing.

'But you didn't say what was wrong with you.'

He'd touched on a raw nerve there. Those concealing eyelids flickered up, fast but hesitant, and the blue eyes flashed one swift, wary and defensive look in his direction before she stared down again, focusing on where her hands were twisting in the protection of the quilt, revealing an uncertainty she didn't want him to know about.

Yesterday he had wanted to hate her. It had been *easy* to hate her when she had come sneaking onto the island like a thief in the night, invading the world he had built around Marco since she had walked out on them. He hadn't wanted to listen then.

And hatred—hatred and rejection—had been uppermost in his mind when she had declared to his face the truth of why she was here. That she had come to try to claim Marco. Then his rage had been like a red mist in front of his eyes and he had had to turn away from her rather than give in to the murderous fury that boiled inside him.

He wished he still felt like that. To stay feeling that way would have been so much simpler. It would have made things so much more easy and straightforward. This woman had walked out on their marriage, their child so carelessly and selfishly, without even a backward look. Now she was back, walking into the life he had made without her.

And demanding her son.

No!

Even now the roar of rejection was wild and savage inside his head. It obliterated every other consideration in a storm of savage feeling. It felt wonderful, simple, strong—and right.

But then she had fainted. She had turned white, all the blood draining from her face, had just seemed to shrivel up at his feet. She had lain there unconscious and he had had to kneel beside her, checking her pulse, her breathing, her temperature. Knowing that he had to take her somewhere more comfortable, he had had to bend to lift her up…

And that was when everything had changed.

'No, I didn't say,' Lucy flung at him now. 'Are *you* saying you want to know what happened? Do you really…'

She had to break off the question as a knock came at the door. Of course—Tonia with the food he had told her to prepare for Lucy. Food it was obvious she needed.

'Eat your breakfast,' he commanded gruffly. 'Then we'll talk.'

'I want to talk now…' Lucy protested, struggling to sit up enough to take the tray on her knees without letting the covers fall down at the same time.

The sudden pretence of modesty set his teeth on edge so that with a muttered imprecation under his breath, he strode to the wardrobe and wrenched open the door. Snatching a white robe from a hanger inside, he tossed it in Lucy's direction, gesturing to the maid to leave at the same time.

'You need to eat.'

Now she was trying to pull on the robe while still balancing the tray.

'*Dio santo!*'

Clamping his jaw tight shut against the irritation that almost escaped him, he lifted the tray again, carrying it to the small table set in the bay window and dumping it down. Then he moved back to the bed, taking the robe from her while she still struggled with it and holding it open for her to get into it.

'If it will speed up the process, I assure you I am not looking,' he told her satirically when she still hesitated.

He didn't have to look—the memory of every inch of her body was etched onto his brain. And not just from last night, when he had taken the shirt and jeans from her unconscious body. No, the memories he had were from the time when they had been together. When her warm, smooth skin and long slender limbs had been a source of endless delight. When he had known the scent of her, the taste of her, every intimate inch of her.

Six months had not been long enough to erase the memories that could still torment him. And last night just knowing that she was back in his life had badly disturbed his sleep, making him twist and turn in the grip of erotic dreams. Eventually he had woken in a tangle of bedclothes, soaked in sweat and breathing as hard as if he had run a marathon.

So now, even with his closed lids concealing his eyes, he could still see her in his thoughts, still feel the heat of her body as she slipped into the robe he held for her. And the soft slide of her hair over his fingers as she flicked it back, the clean, deeply personal scent of her skin, intensified by the warmth of the bed she had just left, was a sensual torment, hardening his body into tight and aching demand in an instant. He couldn't stay in the room a moment longer and not give in to the hot demands of his body.

As soon as Lucy had shrugged the robe up over her shoulders and was reaching for the belt he seized the opportunity to head back to the table, pulling out the chair with an unnecessary flourish.

'Eat,' he commanded. 'And then get dressed.'

He knew that he had stunned her, could feel the focus of her eyes on the back of his neck as he headed for the door.

'But you said that we have to talk.'

'Later,' he tossed over his shoulder at her. 'Get some food inside you and get dressed, then we'll take things from there.'

'Dressed?'

Her voice was sharp in a way that was disturbingly close to the edge on his own tongue, shaking him right to the core with the suspicion that she too might have felt the fiercely heated tug on her senses that he had experienced just a few moments before.

'Dressed in what? At least have the courtesy to tell me where you've put my clothes.'

'You'll find all you need in there…'

A wave of his hand indicated the large, carved wooden wardrobe set against the far wall but he still did not let himself pause, didn't even glance back to see if she had registered his response. He needed to get out of here, get himself back under control. Giving in to his most primitive male urges right now would be the worst possible mistake he could make.

But, *madre di Dio,* he was tempted…

'I'll be back in twenty minutes,' he warned on his way out of the door. 'Be ready.'

CHAPTER SEVEN

I'LL be back in twenty minutes, Ricardo had said. *Be ready.*

And the *be ready* had been a command, one that his tone had told her that he expected to have obeyed without question.

A swift glance at the clock told Lucy that well over half of that time was already up and she was no nearer to obeying that autocratic command to be ready than she had been in the moment that Ricardo had strode from the room, obviously not wanting to spend a moment longer in her company than he had to.

At first she'd done as she was told and eaten her breakfast— rather mutinously perhaps, but she'd been really hungry and the savoury frittata had looked and smelled wonderful, as had the coffee and freshly baked bread. It had been too long since she had eaten and after just one bite even the concern over just what Ricardo had planned for her faded in the face of her appetite and she'd wolfed down everything that was on her plate.

She would have liked to have lingered over a second cup of coffee, but already the time was passing and she still had to shower and dress. Just the thought of Ricardo arriving while she was still in the shower was enough to send her rushing into the bathroom and switching on the water.

She felt so much better when she was washed and refreshed, her hair clean and combed clear of the knotty tangles that the wind on the lake yesterday had whipped it into.

She must have looked a real sight, she reflected as she fastened a towel around her and padded back into the bedroom, glaring at her reflection in the big mirror on the door of the wardrobe. With her tangled hair and too pale face without even a trace of make-up, it was no wonder that Ricardo had barely spared her a glance.

She looked nothing like the woman he had married. The woman who, well aware of the fact that she was not the sort of woman that Ricardo Emiliani was usually seen with in the gossip columns of the celebrity magazines, had made sure that she always looked her best for him.

And, if she had needed any extra push in that direction, then the conversation she had overheard in the Ladies at a party shortly after her wedding had made certain that she stuck to her resolve. Hidden in one of the cubicles, she had heard the sneering tones of one of the female guests.

'Not his usual type, is she?'

'Not at all,' another woman had answered. 'But she's been clever. She trapped him by getting pregnant. He'd never have married her otherwise.'

'Not clever enough. Everyone knows he's just waiting till the baby's born and then he'll divorce her. I mean—what does she have to offer a man like Ricardo? She's too plain, too unsophisticated, way too clingy. I give her a year max after she's delivered before he's back playing the field.'

Lucy had made a vow right then and there that she wouldn't cling—ever. She had also vowed that she would always be as groomed and glamorous as the women Ricardo was usually seen with. She…

But that was where her thoughts stopped dead, dying in the

moment that she flung open the wardrobe door. Her hands shook, her heart seemed to stop beating as she stared at the contents in horror, her whole body trembling in the rush of bitter memories.

'You'll find all you need in there…' Ricardo had said, and all she had expected to find inside the wardrobe was the clothing he had taken off her. Just the cotton shirt and jeans, looking lost inside the vast space of the cupboard.

But nothing looked lost. On the contrary, the wardrobe was stuffed full of clothing—skirts, trousers, dresses, tops, even shoes, all crammed into the available space without an inch to spare. So many—most—of the items were still in their cellophane wrapping or the plastic bags that had protected them in the shop, the shoes in their boxes. And all still with the price labels attached, just as they had been brought home after a wild spending spree.

A wild, crazy, mindless speeding spree.

'Oh, my—'

Lucy clamped her hands hard over her mouth to hold back the choking cry of despair that almost escaped her, stinging tears burning at the back of her eyes. But the truth was that she was beyond crying, beyond thinking. She could only stare in horror at the evidence of just how out of her mind she had been.

The shopping expeditions were a blur in her mind. She knew she'd been on them, of course; she hadn't completely lost her memory of that appalling time—she only wished she could. But the details had been gently hazed by the passage of time until now, when she was confronted with the physical evidence of the truth.

Had she really bought all these clothes—hundreds, *thousands* of pounds' worth of clothes? More clothing than she could ever wear in a year—a decade! Some of the items were almost identical—the same style, the same shape—except that they were in a wide variety of colours, one of each in the whole range the shop would have stocked. And not even everything had been unpacked. There were still bags and carriers stuffed in at the bottom of the cupboard, bearing the names of the exclusive stores in which they had been bought, brought home—and left unopened and untouched.

'Oh, dear heaven…'

What had she really been like in those dark, desperate days? And what had it been like for Ricardo, living with her, watching her crazy behaviour? He had already thought she wanted his money—these wild spending sprees could only have confirmed his darkest suspicions.

She slumped against the door, shaking her head in despair.

If she needed any proof of the fact that she had been right to go, to leave when she had done, then it was here before her, with no room for doubt. She had been out of her mind, totally incapable of managing her own life, let alone taking care of her precious baby son.

And did she have any right to stay here now? To come back into Marco's life and turn it upside down when he was so obviously settled and happy with Ricardo? She knew what it was like to be at the centre of a parental custody battle, to be torn and unsettled, tugged this way and that between her father and her mother like a bone between two dogs when they had been going through a bitter divorce. She couldn't do that to her little boy.

Still half-blinded by tears, she reached out and grabbed the first clothes that came to hand, pulling on underwear, a deep pink skirt and a pink and white top without even noticing what she was wearing. If she could get out of here before Ricardo came back…

She was at the door when it swung open in her face, forcing her to step back hastily.

'So you're ready—good…'

Ricardo's dark eyes swept over her assessingly, and she knew the moment that something of the truth hit him from the way that his black brows snapped together in an angry frown and his whole expression changed from approval to forbidding in the space of a single heartbeat.

'Leaving, *cara*?' he questioned sharply, the tone of his voice and the icy glare that accompanied it sending a shiver down her spine. 'I think not.'

'And why not?' Lucy was determined not to let him see how much he was getting to her. 'You can't keep me here.'

'I think you'll find I can.'

'So you're still determined to keep me a prisoner?'

'Not a prisoner, *tesoro*…'

Ricardo's wickedly sensual mouth curled over the word in a way that took it to a point light-years from the term of affection it was supposed to be.

'You'll find no locked doors here, no bolts—no chains.'

To Lucy's amazement he actually stood back, pushing the door wide open and leaving it that way so that she could get past him—and out—if she wanted to.

'I just think you would find it very difficult to get off the island. But, if you want to try, then be my guest. You were always a strong swimmer, as I recall.'

Coming to an abrupt halt, Lucy had a nasty little fight with herself not to sink back against the wall in admission of defeat. She couldn't quite believe it herself, but she had genuinely forgotten that the villa was set on its own little island. The distance between here and the shore was far too great for her to want to risk trying to swim it.

'All right,' she said, her lips and throat stiff with tension. 'You've made your point. But I still don't see why you want me here when earlier you were so keen to get rid of me. Oh, of course...' Realisation dawned as she remembered. 'You're waiting for that explanation. No?' she questioned when Ricardo shook his head.

'No,' he confirmed. 'There is something we have to see first.'

'Something you've decided I must see, you mean,' Lucy shot back and watched as he sighed his exasperation.

'Do not look at me like that. I promise you that this is important.'

'Important in what way?'

'Lucia!' Ricardo raked both his hands through the black silk of his hair, shaking his head in disbelief. 'Must you argue with *everything*? Can you not trust me on this?'

'Trust you?' Lucy scorned. 'So tell me why I should trust you when you have trapped me here, made sure I can't leave unless I swim for it and...'

Her voice trailed off as she suddenly looked into Ricardo's deep dark eyes and caught something there. Something that stilled and held her frozen.

'Trust me,' he said again and the words tugged on something deep inside, twisting around Lucy's heart just when she was least expecting it.

It wasn't rational, it was totally unwise, probably very naïve, but just in that moment she did trust him. So much so that when he took her arm and turned her in the opposite direction, she didn't pull away from his grasp but allowed herself to be directed down the corridor again, towards the other side of the house.

The part of the villa where their suite had been when they had lived here as man and wife.

That set her nerves tingling in apprehension. Not at the thought of what Ricardo might do but the fear of just how she might react if she was forced to go back to that part of the Villa San Felice where she had lived with him as his wife. The part of the villa where she had been at her happiest, she admitted to herself, fighting against the slash of pain that the memories brought. How would she feel if she had to look into the room where she and Ricardo had spent so many wonderful, blissful nights?

Only *physically* blissful, stern reality forced her to remind herself. Any emotional contentment she had felt had been based on a lie. A lie she had told herself just to keep from facing up to the truth. She might have fallen head over heels for her husband, but for Ricardo the marriage had just been one of pure convenience. The fact that it had also put a willing and passionate sexual partner into his bed every night had just been a bonus in his eyes.

'Ricardo…' she tried but he either didn't hear her or refused to acknowledge that he had.

But the twisting nerves in her stomach eased as they rounded a corner and Ricardo took the opposite direction to the one she had been anticipating with dread. The next moment he stopped before a closed door, turned the handle and pushed it open.

Immediately Lucy knew what he was doing and, if she had felt fearful before, now a terrible sense of panic rushed at her with the emotional force of a tsunami. She froze in the doorway, unable to move back or forwards, though she knew from the way that Ricardo's hand gripped her elbow that he was not going to let her escape.

The room was decorated with all the bright pictures, the blue and white carpet and curtains that she had chosen with such joyful anticipation before the birth of her baby. The same huge soft cushions were set on the floor, the same mobile with the cheerful painted animals hung from the ceiling. All this Lucy took in in a single glance. But then her gaze went to the big cot standing against the far wall and every other thought left her head.

'Marco…'

It was just a whisper, barely a thread of sound, and she was amazed that she could get that out past the knot in her throat. Her heart, which had stopped dead in the moment she had recognised the room as the nursery, was now beating so fast and so wildly that she couldn't catch her breath. If it got any worse, then she feared that it might actually burst out of her chest in the rush of emotion that made her head swim viciously.

At her side she was barely aware of Ricardo making a silent gesture with one hand. In response a young woman in a neat uniform, clearly the nanny hired to look after the baby, slipped silently from the room, leaving them alone. And all the time Lucy couldn't move, couldn't speak, couldn't think. She could only stare wide-eyed at the small person lying under the quilt in the cot, his black hair startling against the white sheet.

Marco's eyes were closed and he was fast asleep. One small hand was flung up outside the coverings and his deep breathing made soft snuffling noises as he exhaled.

'Marco…'

It was all that she could manage and she swayed towards him where she stood but didn't dare to try to make a move towards the cot. It was what she wanted most in all the world and yet what she feared in the same moment as she longed for it. Tears blurred her eyes but they were too hot and too bitter to give release to them. She almost felt as if they would burn down her cheeks like acid if she actually let them fall and flow.

And all the time she was so desperately aware of Ricardo standing next to her, still and silent, just watching her, his dark eyes observing and noting everything.

She didn't know what he was thinking and, quite frankly, she didn't care. All she knew was that her son—her baby—was just across the room from her and she didn't know how she could get to him, or even if she dared to try.

'Marco…' she said yet again. Then, as Ricardo's stillness and silence got through to her once more, she cleared her throat and forced the words out.

'"Something we have to see", you said,' she croaked in reproach.

'This is what you came for, isn't it? You wanted to see Marco.'

Lucy could only nod silently, the one accusing outburst she'd managed seemed to have drained all her strength so that she couldn't find any words to answer him.

What was happening here? What was in Ricardo's mind? Why had he brought her here like this—to see her baby—and yet once again be so near and yet so far? How had he come from *Not while I live* to actually leading her to the nursery, dismissing the nanny?

He couldn't be so cruel as to let her see Marco, come within touching distance of the baby and…

'Then go and see him,' Ricardo said, stunning her.

He wasn't touching her, wasn't doing anything to push her forward or to hold her back either. The hand that had been on her arm had dropped to his side and he was standing back, waiting—and watching. She could feel the burn of his gaze on her face so fiercely that she didn't dare to turn to meet the darkness of his eyes.

'I can't…'

This couldn't be happening. Not after she had dreamed of

it for so many weeks, ever since the doctors had told her that
she was fine now. That they were sure she could handle things,
and that she was no longer a danger to her baby or to herself.
Without that assurance she would never have dared even to
try to make contact. But she had wanted this moment so much
that now she could not believe it was actually real.

'Yes, you can.' Ricardo's voice was surprisingly soft,
though still without any trace of emotion in it. 'He's real,
Lucia. Our baby—our son. You can…'

'No, I can't!' It was a cry of raw pain, dragged from her as
if it was tearing her soul out by the roots, leaving her bruised
and bleeding deep inside. 'I can't—'

'Have you come all this way to give up now? Whatever else
I thought of you, Lucia, I never considered you a coward.'

Coward! If he had meant to sting her into action—and
Lucy strongly suspected that he had—then it worked. Before
she had time to think, rejection of that accusation had pushed
her forward, the impetus driving her to the side of the cot
before she had time to think.

And from the moment that she looked into her baby's
face there was nowhere else she could look at all. Nothing
else that mattered.

'Oh, Marco…'

Sinking down onto the floor beside the cot, she curled her
fingers around the white-painted bars and just stared, seeing
the way that the baby's chest rose and fell, the curl of his
lashes onto the soft cheeks, the faint bubble that formed at his
lips as he breathed.

'Darling…sweetheart…'

And looking was just not enough. Slowly one hand
uncurled itself from the bars, then slid between them, reaching
out towards where Marco lay. With soft fingers she touched

his cheek, then curved her palm around the top of his small head, resting gently on the fuzz of jet-black hair. It seemed to fit so perfectly, and yet it was so different from the times that she had held him before that it made a terrible sorrow at all that she had missed clog up her throat.

'He's so big…' she choked out, fighting the tears.

The silence that greeted her words tugged hard on her nerves, making her tense suddenly where she sat. Ricardo still stood in the doorway; he didn't seem to have moved a muscle. And it was the fact that he was so very still, so totally, dangerously still that tightened every muscle in her body, made the tiny hairs at the back of her neck lift in a shivering, fearful moment.

He was as still as some fierce hunting predator might be while watching his prey wander innocently on the plains before him. He was just waiting, poised ready to move— ready to pounce.

'Strange…' he said now, and for all it was so quiet, so apparently calm, his tone did nothing to ease the sensation of being hunted down. If anything, it made it so much worse, twisting her nerves in a sense of intuitive terror, though of what she had no idea. 'He still seems so small to me. But then I see him every day—so I expect that the difference between when you saw him last and now is so much more pronounced.'

Could what he said be any more pointed? Could he do anything more to drive home the point that he had been here with Marco all the time, while she had abandoned their baby when she had walked out?

Slowly she raised her head, lifted her eyes to meet his, and when she saw the dark opaqueness of his gaze she knew what was happening.

He was testing her. She was under total scrutiny, like some

small defenceless creature dissected on a laboratory table and then placed under the microscope. He was testing her, and she had no idea whether what she was doing was the right thing in his eyes or exactly the opposite.

As she fought to control the fearful shudder that took her body by storm, she saw the sudden change in his face and knew that the predator had finally grown tired of watching and waiting.

He had decided to pounce.

CHAPTER EIGHT

'ALL right…'

Ricardo had thought that he would have to force himself to keep his voice calm, his body still. He had anticipated that at this point he would have to struggle with himself not to lose the tight grip he had on his emotions and to control the rising rage that was welling up inside him. But instead it all seemed suddenly so much easier than he had ever anticipated.

It was as if the time he had spent standing unmoving, just waiting and watching, had fixed his limbs in place so that he couldn't move them even if he wanted to. And at the same time a storm of ice had entered his mind, his veins—his heart—freezing them so that there was no feeling, no response in any of them.

He didn't even feel anger any more. Only the icy certainty that there was something he really needed to know here. The suspicion had been planted in his thoughts yesterday and it had taken root there, growing stronger overnight, with each moment of today. On some deep, instinctive gut level he had known that there was something missing in the story Lucy had told him. And what he had just seen had confirmed it.

He had had to see Lucy with Marco. Had to see if the callous indifference she had displayed in her leaving note had been true. And so he had brought her here to see how she reacted.

And she hadn't behaved at all as he had expected.

'I think it's time we got to the truth. The real truth—nothing else. You said you were ill—but there's more to it than that.'

Her behaviour had not been that of the monster mother he had created in his mind. There had been real pain, real fear in that *I can't*... And the way that she had cradled the baby's head had been so needy and yet so desperately gentle, making it plain that she was anxious not to disturb the little boy's sleep.

So what the hell had driven her away, leaving only that appalling note behind?

'What happened to you, Lucia?'

'I—'

She opened her mouth to speak, then closed it again, looking from his face to that of the sleeping baby and then back again. And the way that she had lost all colour from her face until her skin looked bloodless pushed him forward into the room, holding out his hand to her to help her up.

'There is a sitting room just through here—we can talk there. That way we will hear Marco if he stirs.'

'Thank you.'

Did she know what it did to him when she looked up into his face like that, with those soft blue eyes so wide and clear? And the touch of her hand in his had a kick that tightened every nerve in his body, sending stinging electrical sparks running up his arm straight to his heart so that it jerked in instinctive reaction.

Just who was this woman who had been his wife? Still was, on paper. It seemed as if in the single day since she had come back into his life she had been half a dozen diverse characters, none of whom he recognised from the Lucy he had first met. The Lucy he had married. Here and now she was like a completely different person from the hard-faced creature who only yesterday had flung in his face her certainty that she would walk away with a large proportion of everything he possessed.

That, and Marco too.

The nanny's sitting room was a small, comfortable area off the main nursery. There was a settee and armchairs, a tiny kitchenette at the far side of the room. Lucy followed him silently into it, not hesitating or pulling away, though her head turned back towards the cot where the baby lay.

'You will see him again,' Ricardo told her gruffly.

'You promise?'

When she looked at him like that he would promise her anything. But that was the way he had been caught before, when he had let what he had believed was her innocent beauty lure him into her bed.

It would do no harm to promise this much. She would see Marco again; he could guarantee that. Any more would depend on what she told him now.

'I promise,' he said and watched some of the tension seep from her body, the tight mouth loosening, the way she held her shoulders easing.

'Thank you,' she said again and the faint tentative smile that accompanied the words caught on something raw deep inside and twisted hard.

'Save your thanks,' he muttered roughly, 'until I've done something to deserve them. Would you like a drink? Coffee?'

'Some water, perhaps.'

A drink would be a good idea, Lucy acknowledged. Her voice had croaked embarrassingly on her words. If she had to tell him the whole of her story, she was going to need some help.

She did have to tell him, she knew that. There was no going back now. For better or for worse, everything had to come out.

'Your water.'

Ricardo's voice sounded harshly from close by, startling her eyes open so that she looked up and straight into his darkly watchful face, seeing herself reflected, tiny and pale-faced in the polished blackness of his eyes. Blank, unreadable eyes. Eyes that gave nothing away.

And suddenly it was as if she had slipped back through time, back to the moment when she had first arrived at this villa after their wedding. The speedboat had ferried them from the shore across to the island and as they'd stepped ashore she had slipped and almost lost her footing. Immediately Ricardo had moved forward and caught her before she could fall, swinging her up into his arms and carrying her along the wooden jetty that led to the wide stone steps up to the house. As he'd lifted her over the threshold into the villa itself he had suddenly looked down into her eyes, his own deep and dark and totally inscrutable, revealing nothing at all about his thoughts or his feelings.

'Welcome home, wife,' he had said.

Then, as he had let her slip to the floor, he had pressed the palms of his hands, big and warm and strong, to the front of her dress, below which the baby she was carrying—the baby that would eventually become Marco—was as yet just a tiny curve to her belly.

'Welcome, mother of my child.'

It had been in that moment that she had realised that she had fallen desperately, irrevocably in love with this man who was now her husband. But only her husband of convenience, married purely for the sake of that baby.

As the mother of his child, she was welcome in his home. As the mother of his child, his home became her home. But only as the mother of his child. For herself, and in herself she had no place here at all.

'Lucia—your water.'

Cold moisture beaded the sides of the glass Ricardo held out to her and as she took hold her fingers slipped, sliding up against his hand where he held it. The contrast between the coldness of the glass and the warmth of his skin was a shock, startling her and making her nerves fizz as if a bolt of electricity had shot up her arm.

And from the way that those dark eyes burned into hers it was obvious that Ricardo had felt it too. Just for a moment as their gazes locked she felt that he was about to say something—she could almost feel the words in the air. But then he apparently had second thoughts and stepped away again to move to the door and check on Marco. The baby was still sleeping soundly so Ricardo turned back, pushing his hands deep into the pockets of his trousers as he leaned against the wall.

'So,' he said flatly. 'The truth…'

Which was guaranteed to tighten Lucy's throat even more.

Lifting the glass to her mouth, she took a swift, deep gulp of the cooling water as she tried to collect her thoughts. She wished that Ricardo would move somewhere else or that he would come and sit down. Standing there, so tall and lean and dark, he seemed to tower over her oppressively, dominating the room and tightening every one of her muscles just to look at him.

'Why…' Her throat clenched and she had to take another gulp of water. 'Why did you bring me here?'

The look he gave her said that that was a question that didn't need answering but all the same he drew in a long, deep breath and then looked her straight in the eyes.

'I wanted to see you with Marco—how you would react. How you would be when you met him for real.'

So she had been right. He had been testing her. The atmo-

sphere she had sensed in the room earlier had been real and
not the product of her overheated imagination.

'And what did you find out?'

'That you lied.'

It was the last thing she had expected but as she opened her
mouth to refute the accusation he ignored her attempt at protest.

'You lied in that note you left when you said you wanted
your freedom—at least when you said you wanted your
freedom from Marco. So something else took you away. You
said you were sick—what was wrong?'

'I wasn't exactly sick…' Lucy hedged. 'It was more like
a…a breakdown.'

She had his attention now. Those dark eyes couldn't have
burned any stronger, or been more fixed on her face.

'A mental breakdown?'

If there had been any hint of shock or horror in his voice
then she might not have been able to answer him but the truth
was that his tone was completely controlled, totally matter-
of-fact. So much so that it was only just a reaction.

'Yes…'

She nodded, keeping her eyes locked with his. That steady
black gaze never wavered, never moved. Instead, it stayed
fixed on her, probing deeper and further with every breath
that she took.

'You were depressed.'

'You could say that.' Lucy's voice was shaky, her weak
attempt at laughter even more so. She knew from his quick
frown that her laughter seemed out of place but she just
couldn't hold it back. *Depressed* seemed such an inadequate
word for what she had been through. She had barely known
who she was or what she was doing. And the world had seemed
like a dark, empty cavern, one that she couldn't find her way

out of, no matter how she'd tried. 'Though depressed sounds like the way you'd describe it if you lost a job or your dog died.'

'Not true depression. And if you had a breakdown, then that's what you must have suffered.'

Looking up into Ricardo's face, Lucy blinked hard at the unexpected note in his voice. She hadn't anticipated such sympathy. Was it possible that he might understand after all?

'It was horrible.' She shivered at the memory. 'The whole world seemed black and I didn't know how to make myself get out of bed every day.'

And knowing what she had done to Marco, that by running away she had probably lost him, and the man she'd loved, for ever, had made things so, so much worse. The future had stretched ahead of her, bleak and cold and empty, and she hadn't known how she was going to cope. If it hadn't been for the care of a kind and understanding doctor, the support of therapists, she didn't know how she would have survived.

'There didn't seem to be any point in going on. Any reason to—'

She broke off sharply, startled into awareness of the way that Ricardo had suddenly abandoned his position against the wall and had come close, his fingertips resting lightly on her arm.

'Don't...' he said quietly, pulling her out of the dark fog of her memories.

'Ricardo...' Her voice was all over the place, shaking and quavering in a way that she just couldn't control. And she felt so cold...so horribly cold. She was shivering as if she were in the grip of some horrible fever.

'Give that to me.'

It was only when Ricardo's hand came out and eased the glass from her clenched fingers that she realised how tightly she had been gripping it. She had been holding it so firmly that when her hand had started to shake the water inside the glass had swirled around, slopping over the side and splashing onto the pink linen of her skirt, marring the fine material with ugly dark patches.

She remembered buying this skirt—at least, she thought she did. It had been one of the things she had found on one of the first trips she had made away from the villa a couple of weeks after Marco had been born. She had left him with his nanny and had called Enzo, who took care of and piloted the motorboat, to take her across the lake to the shore. And there she had taken the car into Verona, where she had shopped, hunting for something—anything—that would make her feel more human. Something that would make her feel more alive, more in control of herself and her life.

And something that would make Ricardo look at her like a woman he desired once again.

Without the glass to hold, her hands were shaking even more and when she clasped both of them together on her lap they still kept shaking, shuddering where they lay on the pink skirt. With a terrible effort she twisted them together even more tightly, whimpering faintly when it had no effect.

'Lucia…'

Ricardo's hand, cool from the cold glass, came over both of hers, holding them, stilling them. But he still couldn't calm the waves of despair that were taking her body by storm, making it tremble and shake convulsively.

'Lucia, no,' Ricardo said quietly, calmly. So calm in contrast to the way she was feeling that it stopped her heart for a moment as she tried to take it in. 'There is no need for this.'

'You don't understand…'

Somehow she managed to get the words out, though her voice was as jerky and uneven as her heart.

It was his closeness that was doing that to her. He had slid down now from where he had been sitting on the arm of the settee and onto the cushions beside her. She could feel the warmth of his body, of the long, strong thigh that was pressed close up against hers. And she drew in the scent of his skin with each uneven, ragged breath. The width of his chest in the deep red shirt, the buttons opened at the throat, was level with her eyes, just a hint of dark curling hair revealed in the open neck, and she longed to be able to rest her head against his strength, draw new courage from him. But the distance between them, the yawning emotional chasm that separated her, would always hold her back.

'Oh, but I do.'

To her consternation, she found that Ricardo had somehow seemed to read her mind, to know just exactly what she needed. His strong arms folded round her, drawing her close. At first she tensed, trying to resist. But then the sense of loneliness overwhelmed her and she yielded, soft and yearning, against him.

Her head rested on the hard wall of his ribcage, the steady, thudding beat of his heart pounding under her cheek. She could feel his chest rise and fall with every breath he took and she felt, dangerously, as if she had come home.

Ricardo smoothed one hand over the length of her hair, sliding down her back, raising every tiny nerve in response. The warmth of his palm against the skin of her neck made her heart jolt at the feel of it and a moment when those caressing fingers slid briefly in at the scooped neck of her shirt had her breath catching sharply in her throat. The hard strength of his body was against one breast and as the stroking arm brushed against the other with every slow, gentle movement her nipples tightened in stinging response to the sudden waking need low down between her legs.

'I understand so much better than you could ever believe,' Ricardo murmured, the deep rumble of his voice drowning out the involuntary sigh of longing she had been unable to hold back. 'There's just one thing I want to know.'

Lucy froze against Ricardo's chest. An edge to his voice made her tense in sudden apprehension. The growing sense of warmth and comfort that had been seeping through her body, driving away the chill that had invaded her blood, suddenly seemed to stop and then, shockingly, started to fade again, allowing the shivering cold to start to creep back again.

'I want to know his name.'

She hadn't been wrong about the alteration in his tone, the difference in his mood. It was there too in the sudden change in his position and the way he held her. She was still in his arms, still held close, but it no longer felt like home.

Hard fingers suddenly clamped around her arms, moving her away from him, away from the secure warmth of his lean, hard frame. He held her so that he could look down into her eyes, his dark burning gaze searing her clouded blue one.

'Who the hell is he, Lucia? What's the name of the man who did this to you? The man who drove you to a breakdown when he left you.'

CHAPTER NINE

Who the hell is he, Lucia?… The man who drove you to a breakdown when he left you.

For the first few spinning seconds she hadn't been able to understand what had happened. Ricardo's sharply snapped questions made no sense. She couldn't understand where they came from or why he was even asking them. But then, slowly, reluctantly, she looked back over the conversation and realised the train of thought that Ricardo had been following, the conclusions he had jumped to.

He thought that she had had the breakdown *after* she had left the villa. He really believed—the only way he could possibly see it happening—was that she had run off with another man, leaving him and Marco behind in her determination to start a new life with her lover—his rival.

And then he believed that when that lover had walked out on her, leaving her as she had left him, then and only then had Lucy had the breakdown she had talked about.

'You think that…'

She had stiffened in his arms, pulling away from the warmth and support of his body. And just the tiny movement seemed to take an inordinate amount of effort, bring with it a wrenching pain that was out of all proportion to the distance she put between the two of them.

'You really believe that the only reason I could possibly leave Marco was because there was another man!'

Ricardo didn't need to answer. It was there in his eyes, stamped into the lines of his face. Suddenly, disturbingly, she was seeing her erratic behaviour through his eyes. The excessive spending, the way she had disappeared for most of the day, with no explanation. Had he really thought that she was meeting someone else? That she was having an affair? The thought that she might have put him through that made her shiver inwardly. How could she blame him for thinking so badly of her if that was what he had suspected?

'I can see now that the way I behaved might have made you think that,' she admitted shakily. 'And you don't know how much I regret it if it did. But you have to believe me—there never was anyone else.'

She saw his frown, the way his dark eyes dropped to lock with her own clouded gaze.

'Then why…'

'I wasn't ill—didn't break down after I left here.'

Though leaving Marco had been the last straw. The one that had broken this particular camel's back and driven her in despair and desperation to find a doctor.

'You're saying…'

Ricardo's face changed as realisation dawned. This time his eyes went to the cot where Marco still slept, then came back to her.

'Are you telling me that it was post-natal depression that caused your breakdown? That was why you left?'

Lucy could only nod, her throat too clogged for speech. It was impossible to read the rush of feelings that flashed in

Ricardo's eyes, but she saw the questions there and straight-ened her spine, waiting for them to come. And now he was the one to move away, putting more distance between them.

'That was like no depression I've ever seen.'

'No,' Lucy admitted.

She couldn't hold it against him that he hadn't recognised what even she hadn't known. She had had the doctor to explain it to her. Ricardo had been looking in from the outside.

When he had been there, which wasn't often.

'You were out all the time. Spending money like water.'

'I know—I was hyper. Manic.'

Post-natal psychosis, the doctor had called it. Not just de-pression but the more severe form of the illness, which had literally driven her almost out of her mind. So much so that she had been unable to think straight enough to recognise what was happening to her.

It hadn't helped that her relationship with her own mother had been so difficult. The only time that Janet Mottram had shown any real interest in her daughter had been when she had used the child as a pawn in her personal battle with her ex-husband. And, looking back, Lucy knew that what she had feared most was being as distant and unloving a mother to Marco as Janet had been to her.

And, without anyone to confide in, she had been trapped with her own thoughts. Thoughts that had so frightened and appalled her that there was no way she could have admitted them to Ricardo.

So she had put on a front. A cold, distant front that had driven him away from her even more. And she had succeeded so much better than she could have hoped. From the time that Marco had been born, she and Ricardo had barely spoken to each other. It had been what she wanted but at the same time it had added to the aching inside her, creating a spiral of despair from which she had felt that she would never break free.

'You bought clothes, perfume—clothes you never wore when you were with me.'

And he had thought that she had bought them to make herself look good for someone else.

'All that spending—it was just an attempt at distraction. I didn't even want the clothes half the time.'

And the other half she had wanted them to boost her image, to make Ricardo look at her with the desire he had once shown her. But it had seemed that the women she had overheard had been right. She was not the sort of wife who could hold a man like Ricardo. A man who didn't do commitment. Who was used to having his pick of the most glamorous, most sophisticated women of the world.

If only he would speak—say something. Anything, other than subjecting her to the dark, silent stare that seemed to want to probe right into her eyes, burn its way into her head.

'Heaven knows what you must have thought of me!'

'It was only what I expected,' Ricardo stated flatly. 'Normal female behaviour. Every woman I've known has been out for what I could give her. Why should you be any different?'

How could she fight such cynicism? She hadn't been able to do so when they had been together, so why should anything be different now? Besides which the thought that she still hadn't told him absolutely everything, that there were still things she was holding back, things she could hardly bear to think of herself, sat like a leaden weight in her heart, closing off her throat so that there was no way she could make herself speak.

'And you are well now?' he asked, an edge to his voice that she couldn't interpret and she felt too emotionally adrift even to try.

'The doctors say I am,' she managed stiffly. 'They think all should be well and that I'm not likely to relapse. I would never have come back here if I'd thought…'

'I believe you,' Ricardo said when her voice broke too much for her to go on. He was still so very distant, his deep-set eyes hooded and hidden, but his tone gave her a little cause for hope.

'So if you could see your way to letting me spend some time with Marco…'

And, just at that moment, with amazing timing so that it was almost as if he had heard his name spoken, in the other room the baby stirred and started to whimper faintly, still half asleep.

'Marco…'

Instinct drove Lucy to her feet but she was only halfway there when realisation struck and she froze, grabbing at the settee arm for support as she looked back at Ricardo, meeting the deliberately blanked out expression in his narrowed gaze.

'I…I'm sorry…'

She regretted that as soon as she'd said it. She wasn't sorry at all for reacting automatically to the sound of her child's cry. She might not have been the best mother in the world—she knew she hadn't—but that didn't mean that her maternal instincts had died, swamped by the tidal wave of foul stuff that that rushed over her in the depths of those darkest days. After all, she'd only left because of what she was afraid of. Because of the fear that she might do something dreadful to her little boy. That was those mother's instincts working overtime, not losing their way. And now she was doing exactly the same—responding to the way that her baby most needed her.

The memory of that cry had never left her. In her sleep she would hear it and come jerking awake, sitting up in a rush, eyes wide with horror and fear, needing to find Marco…and knowing he wasn't there. That had been the worst, the most terrible moment of all. The thought that somewhere her baby was crying and she couldn't go to him.

Here and now, she could respond to his call. But at the same time she didn't quite dare to. Not with Ricardo watching and not knowing how he would react if she followed her instincts. He had sworn that she would never take the baby from him, so would he let her comfort the little boy—or would he grab at her arm, to hold her back? Or would he, worst of all, wait until she was at the cot's side, about to take her son into her arms and then snatch the little boy away from her—so near and yet so desperately far again.

'I doubt that you'll understand…but…' Her voice trailed off as she met the burning darkness of his eyes, felt herself flinch under their scorching force.

From the other room came a second more wakeful cry, louder this time, drawing Lucy's eyes in a glance of yearning anxiety towards the door.

'I'll call the nanny,' Ricardo said and the words brought back such a rush of memory that it pushed her response from her mouth before she had had a moment to consider if it was wise.

'No!' she said sharply. 'No nanny! Not now.'

'You were happy enough to leave him in her care before.'

'Did you give me any choice?' Lucy flung at him. 'Did you even discuss it with me? No—you made a unilateral declaration that Marco was going to be looked after by a nanny. It may be the way you were brought up—the norm in your wealth driven world to have your children farmed out to the hired help, but it wasn't what I wanted.'

'I had no intention of having him "farmed out",' Ricardo snapped coldly. 'And it certainly wasn't the way that I was brought up. My mother barely had enough money to feed and clothe me, never mind hire a nanny.'

'Then why did you hire one for Marco? Did you think I wasn't good enough to look after your son, the precious Emiliani heir?'

She didn't believe that his eyes could close up any more, or become any more opaque, but it was like looking into the immovable face of a statute. One that was carved from cold, hard marble.

'That was never my aim,' he said at last and if a statue could have spoken then it would have had just that same stiff, icy voice. 'If you want the truth, I was fool enough to think that you might appreciate some help.'

That cold comment twisted a knife in Lucy's already tender conscience. She'd been so caught up in her own misery that she'd never looked at it from this angle. Now she was forced to face the fact that her own lack of self-esteem had turned what had been an attempt to do the right thing into the exact opposite.

'I'm sorry…' she began but as she spoke Marco whimpered again.

'Your son needs you,' Ricardo said.

'What?'

She hadn't quite caught what he had said. Or, if she had, then she wasn't at all sure that she could possibly have heard right.

'Your son needs you,' he repeated, calm, coldly controlled and totally unmistakable this time. 'You had better go to him.'

She knew that look, that assessing scrutiny. He was testing her again. But which was the right way to react? How could she prove herself to him? And just what did he want her to prove?

She could only go with her instincts. There was no way of second-guessing him.

And, as the whimper turned into a wail and then an

outraged cry, she was left with no choice. She no longer gave a damn what Ricardo thought or felt. It was what Marco needed that mattered. She was out of the sitting room in a rush, bending down over the cot before Ricardo could say a word. And she knew that if he had spoken, if he'd tried to stop her, then she would have ignored him completely.

'Hush little one…it's all right. Mu…'

Her throat closed over the words, choking them off. How could she call herself 'Mummy' after all that had happened? Marco would never understand—and would he even let her touch him?

Painfully aware of the way that Ricardo had moved to the doorway, one strong hand resting against the wood of the frame, she could feel the burn of his eyes in her back as she reached in and scooped up the little boy, lifting him gently. He was so much bigger than the last time she had held him that she felt the unexpected weight of him in contrast to then. That dreadful time when she had felt that she had to give him one last hug, in spite of the fears that were whirling in her head, telling her that she wasn't safe with this precious child. That she had no idea just what she might do.

'Careful, darling…'

Was it just the unfamiliar voice, or would she be completely fooling herself to think that the baby recognised her somehow? Lucy's heart clenched sharply as the little boy's big dark eyes opened wide to stare into her face, his wails and his whole body stilling as she lifted him so carefully.

'That's better, isn't it?'

She prayed that he wouldn't feel the way she was trembling all over. That the twisting of her nerves wouldn't communicate itself to him and upset him all over again. She also hoped that Ricardo wouldn't see the fear in her eyes, the determined effort she was making to hide the way she was feeling and misinterpret it as something else.

'Now, let's see…'

Adjusting the baby in her arms, she caught a telltale whiff that left her in no doubt of something that needed dealing with. She didn't have much experience of caring for her child, but this was something practical she'd done for him, even in the short weeks she'd been with him.

'Oh, so that's the problem! Let's see…'

A swift glance around made it clear just where the changing mat and all the things necessary for cleaning and changing a nappy could be found and she moved towards it, taking Marco with her. She was determined not to look in Ricardo's direction, knowing he was still watching her like a hawk. No doubt just waiting for her to make a mistake, show some hesitation. Something he could criticise. Something he could hold against her.

Well, not this time, Signor Emiliani. She almost laughed as she laid Marco on his back on the brightly coloured changing mat. This was something she knew how to do.

'Let's get you cleaned up…'

Unfastening the sleep suit, removing the dirty nappy, cleaning, was the work of moments. And she enjoyed it—doing this simple task for her baby. Even when Marco waved his arms and legs wildly in the air, wriggling so that it was a struggle to get the nappy on and fastened, she couldn't hold back the soft chuckle of appreciation of his life and energy. Forgetting about the dark, watchful man behind her, she bent her head and blew a loud raspberry on his exposed stomach, revelling in its soft roundness, the uncontrollable giggles that burst from him in response.

Perhaps with Marco at least things could come right.

Maybe in time she could make up to him for the way she had left him. If Ricardo gave her that time, she was forced to add as a movement behind her told her that her husband had left his watching position and come closer.

'That's you done,' she said, pretending she hadn't noticed, determined to ignore him as she fastened the baby's clothes, lifted him carefully, cradled him against her shoulder. 'Now, let's see…'

'Give him to me.'

She'd been expecting it but still it was like a blow to her heart. She'd known he wouldn't give her free rein with the baby, that he was just watching and waiting…

Instinctively her arms tightened around the sturdy little body. Every part of her wanted to shout *no*, to refuse to hand him over. But she knew she had to think of Marco. She must not upset him. And yet she couldn't just give in to Ricardo's demand.

'This isn't fair,' she said, keeping her voice as calm and as quiet as she could manage as she swung round on her heel, turning to face the big dark man behind her.

Over Marco's soft dark head she faced the baby's father with rejection sparking in her eyes.

'You let me hold him, come close to him—the next moment you take him from me. It's cruel and…'

'I'm not taking him from you,' Ricardo stunned her by saying. 'It's midday. Marco usually has something to eat around now.'

A wave of his hand indicated the padded high chair close at hand.

'Why don't you put him in there?'

The slight emphasis on that *you* brought a stinging reproach that she had to admit to herself she deserved. The sharp reminder of just how little she knew about Marco's life and routine twisted a cruel knife in her heart.

'I'm sorry.'

Moving rather clumsily as she adjusted to the unfamiliar weight of her son in her arms, she tried to put Marco into the high chair. Luckily, he seemed prepared to help her and, obviously recognising that this meant food was on its way, began banging on the tray with an enthusiastic hand, slapping his palm on to the surface.

'Da!' he said excitedly, waving the other hand wildly in the air. 'Da!'

He was too young to be talking properly yet, Lucy told herself, fighting with the twist of misery that sound brought her. And, besides, having only ever been spoken to in Italian, Marco was unlikely to be trying to form the word 'Daddy'. But it was another way of bringing home to her how much she had lost by being away from him at this important stage of his life. The pain that cut at her had her digging her teeth down hard into the softness of her lower lip as she fought with the tears that burned at the back of her eyes.

Ricardo bent to wipe the high chair's tray, receiving enthusiastic pats on his face from his son as he did so. Careful cleaning of those grasping fingers followed.

'Here—give him this…'

Ricardo passed her a sliced banana on a plate.

'Just put it onto the tray and let him help himself.'

The small domesticated tasks, the time taken to feed the baby, brought a new and unexpected peace between them. Ricardo passed her the food that the nanny had left prepared and Lucy put it before the little boy, some of the tension seeping from her face, a light switching on in her eyes.

Had he been mistaken or had there been the glisten of tears in those eyes just a moment before? Ricardo found himself wondering. And did she know what it did to him to see the way that her sharp white teeth had dug into the pink softness of her lower lip as she had looked down at their little boy?

He had lost any ability to read her expression, thrown off balance by what he had just learned. He had trusted her once and that had had such shocking repercussions that he had vowed never to do so again. But this was very different. Vicious guilt clawed at him at the thought that his already hardened prejudice against her might have blinded him to the truth, driving him to misinterpret her behaviour after Marco's birth.

He should wait and watch, see what happened, he resolved in the same moment that another more primitive response shook his mental balance even harder.

Dio santo, but he had had to fight with himself not to react on the most basic instinctive level. Every male impulse had urged him to reach out for her and pull her to him. To kiss away the imprint of her teeth in her flesh and soothe it with his tongue. He wanted to taste her again, know the soft sweetness of her mouth, explore the moist interior and kiss them both to the verge of oblivion.

He wanted to tangle his hands in the golden fall of her hair and hold her just so—exactly where he could kiss her hardest, strongest, with the deepest passion.

But there was something else he wanted too. Something that combined with the sensual hunger, taking it and twisting it brutally inside him until, looking across at her, he had to push his hands deep into the pockets of his jeans against the temptation to use them in another, very different way.

She was looking down at Marco, laughing softly as the little boy squished his banana in his hand, obviously revelling in the mess he was making and the feel of it between his fingers. And Marco was watching her, his wide smile a beam of delight as he held up the sticky mess for her to see.

A child and his mother. That was what a stranger looking in through the wide open French windows would see in the scene before them. A child and his mother enjoying the moment, sharing the experience of food and fun, while the father, the husband, looked on and laughed with them.

A family.

That was how it should be. It was why he had married her, after all. Because his child, unlike Ricardo himself, his mother before that, should have two caring parents. And, having seen Lucy with Marco, having heard her story, how could he refuse her—and Marco—that in the future? He had to let her back into their son's life.

And back into his?

The cold stab of anger at the thought was like a blade of ice between his ribs, making him clench his teeth tight against it.

He couldn't blame her for the way she had run out on her marriage if she had been as ill as she had described. The evidence of her feelings for Marco were there before him in a natural warmth that no one could mistake. But where did that leave their marriage?

Was Marco truly all she had come back for or was there more to it than that? She needed money, obviously, because she had admitted that she had none now. So was she back, looking for the means of support that he as her wealthy husband was obliged to provide? Did she really just want to be with her son or was the fact that she was Marco's mother still her key to the luxurious lifestyle for which she had married him?

'Oh, Marco! What a mess!'

Lucy's voice, soft and warm with amusement, broke into his thoughts, shattering them and sending them spinning off onto another tangent entirely. As she bent her head, leaning down towards the little boy, laughing again as he reached up and smeared the fall of her hair with banana, he found that he was once more seeing the scene as someone else might see it.

That person would see a happy family. Not knowing the events that had torn the little group apart, they would assume it was still the perfect setting in which to bring up the little boy.

Which it was. Or once had been.

He had wanted a family for his child. Still wanted it more than he could say. And if he played his cards right then there was a way that he could still make it come true for the future. For Marco.

And if there were other reasons—private reasons—for him wanting to keep things the way they had been, could he admit them, even to himself? He had no wish to let anyone know the way that, after just twenty-four hours, he was once more fighting the irresistible, burningly sensual passion that Lucy's slender beauty had always been able to arouse in him. And certainly he was damned if he was ever going to let Lucy begin to suspect that those feelings were there. Sex and money had been the reasons why they had gone into this marriage that was not a marriage in the first place. And sex and money had been the things that had torn it apart too. Those two dangerous elements had ruined his past. He was not going to let them ruin his future too.

She seemed to have been honest with him. And she truly seemed to want to be back with Marco, for the baby's sake, not for anything she could get out of this, but her concern could easily be faked. Could he really trust her with his beloved son's future? Why should she be so very different from the other women in his past?

The only way to be sure was to test her sincerity one more

time. To make absolutely sure that her reasons for being here were as she claimed. He would offer her the sort of deal that, if she was lying, would surely tempt her into showing her true colours. And the way she responded would tell him all he needed to know.

But if he could get what he wanted out of this situation—if he could keep her here, for Marco's sake, on the terms that suited him—then he would do just that.

CHAPTER TEN

'I THINK he's had enough…'

Lucy bent down to pick up yet another piece of bread that Marco had flung onto the floor, narrowly dodging the plastic mug of milk that landed right beside her as he discarded that too.

'Shall I clean up here and then…'

'Marissa will do that.'

He saw the look she gave him and acknowledged it with a faint inclination of his head.

'She'll take him for a walk too, to get some air. It's better to stick to his routine.'

Ricardo pressed the bell to summon Marco's nanny before wiping the little boy's face and hands with a clean cloth and hoisting him out of the high chair and hitching him on to one hip.

'And we have things we need to discuss.'

'We do?'

But, as she expected, there was no way that Ricardo was going to answer that as he shook his head and concentrated on wiping a stubborn piece of dried banana out of his son's eyebrow, managing Marco's wriggles of protest with an easy skill that wrenched at Lucy's heart.

'Not here.'

Not here. Not now. Not in front of Marco. Lucy added the words he didn't use, acknowledging the cold creeping sense of fear that welled up inside her as she did so.

So was this it? Was this the moment when Ricardo sent her packing? When her all too brief idyll with her little son came to an end and her husband made sure that she left the island?

And if she did, then would she ever see her baby again?

'No…'

Her hands went out to the child in his father's arms, but at that moment the door opened and the nanny she had seen before stepped into the room. After a brief conversation in Italian, too rapid for her to catch, Ricardo passed the little boy to Marissa and turned to Lucy. Something about the look on her face must have hit home to him because, as he took her elbow to turn her away towards the door, he bent his head and spoke swiftly, close to her ear.

'I promised,' he said roughly and just for a moment she stared at him, not quite understanding.

But then her memory cleared and she had a sudden rush of recollection. Ricardo saying, 'You will see him again,' and the conviction in his words that had had her believing him on that when she couldn't trust him on anything else.

And so she didn't fight but let herself be led from the room, with a long lingering glance back at the little boy who had taken over her heart without a chance of ever letting go.

He had always had her love, of course. It was just that her illness had blurred that love and preyed on her fears of not being a good enough mother. The thoughts she had experienced had been the depression, not the reality. She could see that now. But, at the time, lost and lonely, even if never alone, she had not been able to cope.

Now she knew the depth of her love, the way it had always

been there underneath all the horror and the misery. So how would she cope if Ricardo was once more going to deny her access to her child? Could he do that? And, if he did, then how would she ever be able to afford to fight him in the courts if she had to?

'Where are we going?'

'Just here…'

Ricardo pushed open a door to his left, in a position that Lucy recognised. Her heart sank as she walked into the room he had opened, the setting making it plain that her husband had nothing kind or considerate on his mind. His island home's office, with its dark wood furniture, the big L-shaped desk, the array of computer equipment, was a place for business deals, for cold-blooded decisions with nothing of the heart about them.

'Wouldn't you like to sit down?' Ricardo waved a hand in the direction of a chair, one of three gathered around a small coffee table set in the window overlooking the bay.

'Will I need to?'

His beautiful mouth twisted at the sharpness of her response and he met her attacking tone with a half shrug of one of his broad shoulders.

'It depends on how you're going to react to getting everything you wanted.'

'What?'

That nearly did take her legs from under her and she had to reach out for the back of a chair to support herself as the shock hit home.

'You'd do that?' Her voice shook in disbelief.

'Why not?'

This time he shrugged both shoulders, dismissing her stunned question as totally unimportant.

'It's only money. And I can soon make more.'

Only money.

Lucy's fingers had to clench tight over the back of the chair to keep her from letting her trembling give her away. And at the same time she felt her jaw tighten hard against the impulse to let a cry of distress escape. Of course. *Only money.* Did she really think that Ricardo was going to let her walk out of here with Marco? Simply hand the baby over to her and let her go?

Never in a million years.

But she had hoped for *something*. For a hint of recognition that he had recognised how ill she had been to leave her child, that he had seen how she cared for her little boy. A suggestion that he would let her see Marco—have some sort of access to the baby.

'In return for a quick and quiet divorce, I will give you a small fortune,' Ricardo stated bluntly. 'Enough cash to keep you in luxury for many years, without raising a hand to do a thing.'

He moved round to the other side of the desk, pulling out a drawer and snatching up a cheque book from its interior. Tossing it down onto the desk, he flipped it open, grabbed a pen and started to write. Firm bold strokes of the pen wrote numbers, words—and finished it all off with the slashing force of his signature, firmly underlined.

'I don't…' Lucy began but the sound of the cheque being ripped from the stub drowned her attempt to speak. And when he tossed the paper towards her, landing on the edge of the desk where she could see it, all the strength in her vocal cords evaporated in a sense of shock as hard and cruel as if he had actually punched her in her chest, driving all the breath from her body.

It couldn't be true. She had to be seeing things. Either that or Ricardo was playing with her. A small fortune, he had said.

There was nothing small about the amount on the cheque in front of her. It was an enormous amount—an obscenely large amount. More money than she had ever seen in her life. And Ricardo had tossed it at her as if it were a donation of a few pounds or so.

'You don't mean this.' The hand that she used to point at the cheque was trembling in bewilderment. She could barely read the figures clearly because of the disbelief that was blurring her eyes. You can't mean it.'

'Why not? Isn't it enough?' His eyes challenged her to object.

'It's enough for any human being—but it's not what I want.'

'If you want a divorce, then that's all that's on offer.'

It was that word—*divorce*—that felt like a slap in the face. But then he had made no secret of the fact that he wanted her out of his life permanently. The momentary kindness and understanding he had shown her earlier had misled her. She had thought they had come close to at least the beginnings of an understanding. And that had distracted her from the cold-blooded declaration he had made the night before.

How much will you take to leave now, get out of here—and stay out of my life for good?

Taking her silence as agreement, Ricardo jabbed a finger onto a button on the phone, not even looking at her. Speaking in fast Italian, he was obviously issuing instructions. She caught the name Enzo, the word *nave* and could only assume that the order had gone out to prepare the motor launch. He was really determined to get rid of her as quickly as possible. Which put her right in her place. Paid off, dealt with, dismissed from his thoughts. And about to be divorced by the sound of it. So much for his promise that she would see Marco again.

'Your boat is waiting.'

Could his voice get any colder? Could the long body

express hostility any more clearly than the way he stood, rigidly upright, half-turned away from her as if he couldn't wait to move on? Lucy felt a volatile blend of anger and pain well up inside her, pushing her into unguarded speech.

'No—*your* boat is waiting. The boat you've decided I should take. You never even waited for an answer...'

'So tell me, Lucy, what would you have said if I had asked you? Last night you were so determined to get away from here. Now are you telling me that you want to stay?'

She didn't dare to answer that truthfully. In fact her response was so clear and strong in her mind that she lowered her eyes, afraid that the truth would show in her gaze. It seemed that since she had first made her way onto the island— was it really less than twenty-four hours ago?—she had been on a wild roller coaster of emotions, shooting up and down with dizzying force and speed, never quite knowing which was true and which was safe.

Safer. None of the choices before her had been really *safe*. Last night she had been finding her way, groping blindfolded through the pitch-darkness, with only vaguely formed ideas of what she wanted most, and little understanding of how to approach things. Now she knew exactly what she wanted. She wanted to be a mother to her child and...

It was that *and* that made her thought processes stop dead, made her heart jolt in fear and apprehension and had her concealing her eyes and her thoughts from the man in front of her.

She didn't yet know quite what that *and* implied and until she did then she wasn't prepared to reveal the truth to him. Perhaps even then—perhaps even more than ever then—she would need to conceal the facts from him.

'I don't want to stay here but I do want to be with Marco. I want my son.'

It was the perfect summer afternoon, with the sun streaming in through the window, beyond which the lake water sparkled clear and blue in the light, but when Ricardo's face closed up like that it seemed to drain all the warmth from the atmosphere, dim the light, as if a cloud had passed in front of the sun.

'And you know that I would rather die than let you take him from me.'

'I want my rights as his mother... And, before you tell me that I gave those up when I ran out on him, I defy you to take me to court over it! We'll see what a judge has to say when I explain how things happened.'

'So you would fight for him?' He actually sounded pleased that she had challenged him on this. 'I was beginning to wonder.'

It wasn't that she hadn't been prepared to fight for Marco before. More that, until now, she hadn't been sure that she was the right person to do so. Until she had actually spent time with Marco, touched him, held him, felt the heavy warmth of his little body, inhaled the scent of his skin, that she had known this was what she had to do. That she could no longer live without her baby in her life.

'But, be warned, I'll fight right back. I'll see you in court if I have to.'

'You'd use the fact that I was ill against me?'

'What sort of monster do you think I am? But because I understand that you were ill it doesn't mean that I am going to hand my son over to you without a thought. If I have to fight you for custody then I will and I warn you, Lucy—I intend to win.'

Tension was tying Lucy's over stretched nerves into painful knots. Deep inside she quailed at the prospect of a court battle with Ricardo and the legal team that his wealth would bring him. And the truth was that she couldn't fault the way Marco's father had cared for the little boy. The thought of taking the baby from his father tore at her heart.

'Ricardo, neither of us wants this—surely it doesn't have to be this way? I was the subject of a battle between my parents, both of them wanting me, both of them using me just as a pawn in their private battle. I don't want to do that to Marco.'

'And I don't want the Emiliani name dragged through the gossip columns, my private life exposed. But Marco is my son. I didn't go through a marriage I didn't want just to see you take him from me and turn me into an absentee father.'

'And I don't want to be an absentee mother either…'

What had she said to put that sudden gleam of dark satisfaction into those black eyes? It looked almost as if she had done exactly as he had wanted. Lucy had the sudden, deeply uncomfortable feeling that she had been manoeuvred into a corner, checkmated somehow, and she hadn't even seen it happen.

'Then it seems that there is only one way to handle this.'

'There is? And what's that?'

To her astonishment, Ricardo leaned forward and snatched up the cheque from where it still lay on his desk between them.

'Look at that,' he said and, totally bemused, Lucy let him push the slip of paper into her unresisting hand.

'A small fortune,' he said, his voice disturbing in its icy intensity. '"Enough for any human being". And it's yours—if you leave.'

He saw the way that her head came up, the defiant words forming on her lips to fling his offer back at him and the faintest flicker of something that was almost a smile curled the corners of his mouth.

'Or…'

If Ricardo's tone had been glacial, then his eyes seemed to sear right to the core of her soul.

'You can have it the way you want it—if you stay here.'

Unnerved and mentally armed for a fight as she was, Lucy at first didn't catch the apparent concession. But when she did it was with a sense of shocked realisation.

'Stay?' she queried uncertainly. 'For how long?'

Ricardo's stony gaze burned into her, unflinching, unyielding.

'For good.'

One arrogant wave of his hand towards the window indicated where the boat waited, Enzo standing at the wheel, the subdued pulse of the engine seeming unnaturally loud in the silence. Another took in the room they stood in, the whole of the beautiful villa.

'There is your choice. The boat or the island. If you want to talk about this, then you stay here. If you want to leave, then the subject is closed. For ever.'

'But…'

Lucy's thoughts were spinning in a new and different kind of panic. She had the terrible feeling of being trapped. She had been manoeuvred into a very tight corner and it seemed that there was no way out of it.

'You can't keep me here!'

'No, but Marco can.'

'I…don't understand.'

Despairingly, Lucy shook her head, unable to make sense of what he was saying.

'It's quite simple. If you want the money, then you leave— get on the boat and let Enzo take you wherever you want. But if you want contact with Marco—and I think you do—then you stay here.'

'You'd let…'

'But, in that case, then the money is no longer yours. I'll stop the cheque…'

'You won't need to.'

The rush of delight at the thought that he might let her stay was dizzying in its force. How would this work? Perhaps Ricardo had some idea of letting her replace the nanny, or at the very least act as back-up… She didn't know and didn't care. She wanted to stay.

Without thinking, she took the cheque in a firm grip and ripped it into a thousand tiny pieces, tossing them wildly in the air so that they scattered around their heads, floating down softly to the ground like a fall of confetti. Drifting around Ricardo's dark head, several tiny white pieces lodged in the silk of his hair, on the broad straight shoulders, settling softly. He barely spared them a glance, his dark-eyed gaze still locked with hers as he watched her response with cool, distant assessment.

And it was in that moment, as she recalled another day, when the confetti had been real, when the tiny coloured pieces of paper had been thrown around them as they'd emerged from the church after their wedding, that her heart gave a painful lurch of realisation. Then, just as now, the confetti had fluttered around them, landing on Ricardo's hair and shoulders. She remembered how on that occasion he had shaken his head in impatience, sending the delicate pieces of paper flying once again as he'd rid himself of the tiny symbols of luck and love.

This time he was still and unmoving, his eyes seeming blank as they looked into her face. And it was that complete lack of expression that made her stomach clench on a cruel twist of apprehension.

'Are you sure?' he asked, his voice as cold as his expression.

'Totally.' She couldn't afford to let him see any doubt in her face, hear it in her tone.

'You will stay?'

'I'll stay.'

She had no alternative. No other alternative she even wanted to consider.

She had already run from this house once and she knew that she couldn't do it again. Then she had known that her heart was being torn in two at the thought of leaving her child behind but she hadn't been able to feel it. The misery that her life had become had battered her brain so badly that it was numbed by the bruising. Today, with her reunion with Marco so fresh and clear in her mind, the scent of his skin on her clothes, her arms still warm from holding him, she felt every dreadful raw, tearing sensation that threatened to break her heart into pieces, leaving her shattered and destroyed.

'*Buono…*'

Once more the phone was in Ricardo's hand.

'You will not be needed today, after all.' He spoke to Enzo but his eyes were on Lucy.

Beyond the window, Enzo leaned forward and turned a key, switching off the boat's engine. The silence that descended was sudden, still and very, very taut, stretching Lucy's nerves until she winced in distress. And in the silence she suddenly realised that she had agreed to stay and yet she had no real idea just what she was agreeing to.

'Just one thing,' she managed, the dryness of her constricted throat making the words come out as a rough-edged croak. 'There's something I need to clear up. If I'm staying…how am I staying? On what terms? Will I be a replacement for the nanny or…'

Silhouetted against the window, Ricardo was just a dark figure against the brightness of the afternoon sun. The sun that was blinding her so that she couldn't read the look on his face, no matter how much she screwed up her eyes.

'I mean…what…who am I staying as?'

'I would have thought that was obvious.' Ricardo's voice was coldly emphatic, totally clear in a way that his expression was not. 'The only way you'll stay in this house is as my wife.'

CHAPTER ELEVEN

THE big ornate clock out in the hallway was striking mid-night, the deep, ominous tones sounding clearly up the curving staircase to where Lucy was sitting in the darkness of the bedroom. Slowly she counted the strokes—anything to distract her mind and give herself something else to think about, no matter how briefly.

'Six…seven…'

It was no good, the distraction didn't work. Her thoughts would keep drifting off to the rest of the day and the time that had passed since Ricardo had decreed that if she stayed at the villa then she did so as his wife.

In the first moments after he'd flung the declaration at her, pure blinding shock had held her frozen, immobile as if someone had aimed a hard blow at her head and left her reeling.

The only way you'll stay in this house is as my wife.

In the silence of the night, the autocratic words sounded so clear that she almost looked around, expecting to see that Ricardo had come into the room to find her and that he was standing right behind her, between her and the door, so that there was no hope of escape.

But the room was as dark and silent as before and the only sound was the faint lapping of the waves of the lake against the shore beyond the partly opened window. She had no idea where Ricardo was or what he was doing.

She hadn't had a chance to speak to him after that one high-handed statement. By the time she had pulled herself together to respond to him, needing to demand exactly what he meant, the phone had rung and Ricardo had swiftly snatched it up.

'Pronto?'

Pausing for a moment, he'd spared Lucy a swift flashing glance before saying sharply, 'I have to take this.'

In case she hadn't got the message, he'd moved to the door and held it open, the pointed dismissal only too clear. There'd been no point in arguing either; his attention was totally focused on the call and she had been completely wiped from his thoughts.

She hadn't seen him since. He had never come back to any part of the house she had been in, but had sent a message to say that he had been called away on business and wouldn't be back until very late that evening.

Well, it was very late now and Ricardo was still not back. She had no idea where he was, or what his plans for her involved.

The only way you'll stay in this house is as my wife.

Why could he possibly want her as his wife, when he had made it plain from the start that he hated her? And… A shiver ran down Lucy's spine that had nothing at all to do with the coolness of the temperature since the sun had gone down…

Just how much of a wife did he expect her to be?

Her whole body felt stiff and cramped and she stretched carefully, easing limbs that had been still for too long. She had fallen fast asleep, lying on the top of the bed as she'd waited for Ricardo's return, and had woken to find the room in darkness and the house silent.

She'd filled the hours between Ricardo's departure and

the onset of evening with enjoying more of Marco's precious company. Upstairs in the nursery flat, still not daring to be on her own with him but, together with the nanny, she had played with him, fed him again. And then, most special of all, she had bathed him and settled him down for sleep in his cosy cot, sitting beside him and singing lullaby after lullaby as she'd watched his eyelids grow heavier and heavier, his breathing slowing until she knew he was deeply asleep.

Even then she had not been able to drag herself away but had stayed, her arms resting on the cot's side, her head on her hands, watching him sleeping for as long as she could. It was only when darkness had finally fallen that she had forced herself from the room and had gone looking for her husband.

Her husband. That, it seemed was what she must now get used to calling him all over again. The man who for his own private reasons wanted her back as his wife—but obviously only on his terms.

And she had yet to find out exactly what those terms were.

So she had come here to the room that Marissa, with carefully disguised curiosity and an obvious struggle not to ask the questions that were burning on her lips, had told her was Ricardo's. Wherever he had been and wherever else he went once he came home, this was where he would have to end up eventually. She had wandered round it, taking in the severe blue and grey, starkly masculine décor that was so unlike the room they had once shared as husband and wife. Here there was little place for comfort, little scope for the softening effects of design or decoration. It was a room that was plain and functional.

It told her nothing new about her husband, nothing about the sort of life he had lived while she had been apart from him. If he had brought other women back to the huge king-sized bed, then it showed no sign of them. If they had been there, then they had been and gone, leaving no scent, no trace behind. To her relief, there was also no sign of any female clothes, no scented toiletries in the bathroom, no make-up scattered in the dressing room. Lucy didn't know what she would have done if she had found them there.

Eventually, the effects of a long stressful day and the build-up of lack of sleep for over a week before that had caught up with her. Telling herself that she would just rest until Ricardo came back, she had lain down on the soft grey and blue covering of the bed, rested her head on the crisp cotton of the pillowcase that still retained some of the most personal scent of Ricardo's skin and hair, inhaled it deeply and letting a single exhausted tear slide down her cheek, she'd fallen fast asleep.

But now she was wide awake again—and Ricardo had not come back. Swinging her legs off the bed, Lucy padded across the thick carpet to the uncurtained window and stared out at the silent, still lake that glistened in the moonlight. From this side of the house she couldn't see the mooring point so she had no idea if Enzo had brought the launch back and Ricardo with him. All the other staff must surely be asleep by now and so...

'What the hell are you doing here?'

The voice came so suddenly and harshly from behind her that she started violently, caught off balance as she spun round in an ungainly movement, gaping at the tall dark figure of the man who stood silhouetted in the doorway.

Her mind had been so preoccupied that she hadn't heard the footsteps on the stairs, or coming rapidly down the corridor. She hadn't known that Ricardo was even in the house until he had appeared without warning and tossed the rough-voiced demand at her, obviously none too pleased to find her there.

'I'm waiting for you,' she managed at last, awkward and un-comfortable. And her unease was aggravated by the way that his dark head went back, his shadowed face tensing suddenly.

'And what the devil gave you the idea that I would want that? This is my room, and what you're doing here at this time of night…'

'But you said that the only way I would stay here would be *as your wife*. Where else should a wife be…but in her husband's room? Isn't that what anyone would expect…would understand from the simple fact that we are married?'

'Anyone would be a fool if they did,' Ricardo growled back. 'This is the last place I expected to see you—the last place I want you to be.'

The effect of the rejection was so powerful that Lucy actually staggered as she stood, reaching out an uncertain hand to grab at the curtains for support. It was only now that she realised how her own feelings had misled her into this situation.

Could see that the hot, hungry need she felt for Ricardo whenever he was near had meant she had put two and two together and come up with an awkward and inaccurate five. She had assumed that he still felt the same about her physi-cally. That at least the burning passion that had brought them together in the first place, rushing them into bed before they had ever had a chance to get to know each other, still blazed unappeased. And it had done—hadn't it? Last night, in her room in the boarding house—and again out on the balcony…

So when Ricardo had declared that he wanted her as his wife then, naturally, she had believed that it was this part of their married relationship that he had wanted to revive.

An assumption that perhaps was not as natural as she had believed.

'But Marissa showed me the way…'

'If Marissa assumed that I wanted you in my bedroom then she overstepped the mark. She…'

'Oh, but that was my fault,' Lucy broke in urgently, terrified that she might get the young nanny into trouble. 'I asked…I thought…'

The words shrivelled on her tongue as Ricardo stepped forward into the room. The light of the moon falling on his handsome face made it look as if it had been carved from marble, tight and cold, his eyes opaque and unreadable.

'You thought that I would want you in my bed?'

His tone made it plain that that had been the furthest thing from his thoughts. Lucy was so grateful for the lack of clear light in the room and the way that it hid the flood of hot colour she could feel rushing up her neck and into her face. Had she got it so terribly wrong?

'You said that if I stayed here then it had to be as your wife.'

'My wife, and Marco's mother.'

Ricardo moved further into the room and flung himself down into a chair at the end of the bed. The change in his position should have made him seem less imposing, less overwhelming in the way that he now no longer towered over her but instead it had the opposite effect. Looking at him as he was now, with his jet-dark eyes gleaming coldly in the wash of moonlight, he seemed even more dangerously distant. If she had ever let herself believe that his decision to allow her to stay had been based on hot-blooded passion then she could no longer think of any such thing.

The man who faced her in this moment looked as if he didn't have a hot-blooded cell in his body. He was all steel and ice, brutal control imposed over any trace of humanity he might have been tempted to show.

'You only want me as Marco's mother?'

What else could there possibly be? the cold burn of his eyes demanded. *What else could I want from you?*

'A child needs two parents—both his mother and his father. That is what I want for Marco. And from the way that I've seen you with him, I can tell that whatever problems you have with our marriage, you don't feel them with him.'

'Yes, you told me about that.'

He'd explained to her in detail, in one of the rare moments of opening up to her about his past. He'd told her then how first his mother, and then Ricardo himself had been turned away from their family's homes because they had been born to the unmarried daughters. The memory of standing on the doorstep as a boy of five with his mother, who had been looking for help, only to have the door slammed in their faces, had burned deep into his soul and made him resolve from then onwards that no one would ever shut him out in that way again. And they would certainly never do it to his child. It was part of what had made him the man he was—ruthless, determined, never taking any help from anyone.

'I understood. It was why I married you.'

'That and the moment that you set eyes on the island, and the villa,' Ricardo returned cynically, lifting one hand in an arrogant flicking gesture that took in their luxurious surroundings, referring to the rest of the beautiful house, the stunning private island.

'Well, yes…' Lucy admitted. 'I saw that this was where your child belonged. That it was our baby's—Marco's inheritance. I didn't want to risk depriving him of this any more than you did.'

What had she said to make him look at her in that way? Why had he suddenly become so still, so focused, with those dark burning eyes fixed on her face as if they wanted to bore

right through her skull and into her mind, read her thoughts—
dig right into the depths of her soul?

'And that is why you married me?'

'Yes, that's exactly why I married you,' she said, fearful
that he might see in her face the evidence of those other very
different reasons why she had agreed to be his wife. The vulnerable, dangerous feelings that she had so longed to see re-
ciprocated. The love that had taken her by storm and left her
unable to bear the thought of life without him. So much so
that she had agreed to a marriage in which she knew that
Ricardo's heart was not involved and never would be.

'So we can work on the same arrangement again.'

'We can?'

Lucy's throat worked convulsively as she swallowed down
the heavy lump that threatened to close it off. From those
moments of half-fearful but—yes, go on, admit it to yourself,
Lucy—half-excited waiting for Ricardo to appear, she now felt
as if she was in a lift that had suddenly plummeted a hundred—
a thousand metres downwards, taking her stomach—and her
heart with it. She had let herself think—let herself imagine—
dream that maybe Ricardo wanted her back as his wife because
in one way at least he couldn't live without her. She'd let
herself think that perhaps he still wanted her in his bed as he
had done before and although the thought had scared her, it had
thrilled in the same moment, sending shivers of reaction along
every nerve that were a form of such nervous exhilaration that
she'd felt as if she had pins and needles all over her skin.

So now the realisation that his plans for her were as cold-
blooded and callous as they had been before made her fight
hard against the bitter tears that burned at the back of her eyes,
clenching her hands in the fall of her pink skirt as she struggled for a control to match his icy composure.

Ricardo was nodding slowly, not seeming to have noticed her tension and the way that she shifted uneasily from one foot to the other.

'Marco needs a mother—you are the natural candidate.'

'Of course,' Lucy confirmed hollowly, unable to drag her voice above a flat murmur.

'But this time things will be different.'

Ricardo placed his hands on the arms of his chair, pushing himself upright with an abrupt movement that took him part way over the floor towards her where she stood at the window. And, as his shadow fell over her, the dark bulk of his body obscuring the light of the moon, she shivered again but this time in pure apprehension, with nothing at all in it of the exhilaration of the time she had spent waiting for him.

'How different?'

To her astonishment Ricardo reached out one hand and touched her cheek, Just once, very softly. It was almost a caress and yet there was something missing. There was such a coldness in it that even when he cupped her cheek there was no sensuality in his touch, no gentleness. It was withdrawn, objective distant. And then he moved again, changing the position of his hand, drawing back all his fingers but one so that there was just one forefinger extended. It barely rested against her cheekbone, a contact and yet not a connection. It was as if he held her prisoner with that one small touch so that she dared not move away in case it tore at her skin to do so.

'If you come back, then this time you will stay. Our child needs you and you will stay with him until he is grown.'

'But of course…'

It was what she wanted so much. Not all that she wanted but a vital, valuable part of it so that she had no hesitation in saying yes.

'This time there will be no running away, no matter what. We will be a couple—at least publicly.'

'Just publicly?' Lucy managed shakily.

Ricardo nodded his dark head so adamantly so that his black hair became tousled, a single lock falling forward onto his broad forehead, making Lucy's fingers itch to reach up and smooth it back, though she knew that he would repulse the gesture violently if she tried.

'All I ask is that you do not bring scandal to my door. That you are discreet. In public we will be seen together—united—the perfect couple. In private it will be different.'

Was he saying that in private he didn't mind if she took a lover? The pain that came from knowing that not only did he not want her any more for himself but that he didn't even seem to give a damn if she slept with someone else, just so long as it didn't get into the papers or create a scandal, was more than she could bear.

'And what about you? Can you manage to be *discreet* as well?' she flung at him, the anguish tearing at her heart making the words cold and harsh in a way that pure anger could never manage.

'I will manage fine,' Ricardo tossed back at her. 'I have already done just that.'

'You have? Really? I don't believe…'

'Why not?' Ricardo challenged. 'Have you heard of anything while you were away? Have you seen my name in the gossip magazines—in the gutter press?'

Which was as good as telling her that he had been clever and careful while they had been apart. That there had been other women—because, of course, being Ricardo, how could there not have been other women?—but that no one would ever find out who they had been.

And no one would in the future. Because it was clear that he planned on keeping his mistresses—*discreetly*—while acting the role of her husband and Marco's father. Because he wanted those other women in his bed when he did not want her at all.

'So…' Ricardo questioned softly. 'What is your answer? Do you agree to this? Are you prepared to act as my wife?'

Did she have any choice? If she gave up on this then she would have to leave and she would be parted from Marco. But if she stayed…

'What do I get out of it?'

'Isn't it obvious?'

What was that look in his eyes, the momentary dulling of their glittering blackness? In anyone else she would have called it disappointment—but in Ricardo?

'You get to be with Marco—to be a mother to your child. And in that time you will live in all the luxury you could want. You will have an allowance that I doubt even you could spend. And when Marco comes of age you will walk away with the full amount—together with all the accruing interest—on that cheque that you so crazily tore to shreds earlier.'

'All of it?' Lucy knew that her eyes had widened in stunned surprise. She couldn't believe the amount that Ricardo was prepared to hand over simply to get his way. 'You'd do all that?'

A shrug of one shoulder dismissed her question as irrelevant.

'My son is worth it,' he said, prowling away to stand staring out of the window at the moonlit lake that surrounded the island. 'The question is, can you say the same?'

'And I suppose you think that this is a very…*civilised* arrangement?' Lucy managed, the words sounding strangled in the tightness of her throat.

'You don't think so?'

'It doesn't seem human to me. I can't imagine why anyone would want to live that way—live a lie.'

Her tone had sharpened on the words and in response she surprised a sudden look in those dark eyes. A flash of something unexpected, as if she had somehow caught him on the raw. It was there and gone again in the space of a heartbeat, leaving her wondering if she had ever really seen it at all.

'Are you saying that it's not what you wanted?' he demanded roughly. 'That you've changed your mind after all?'

'No, that's not what I'm saying.'

'You will stay?'

'I'll stay,' Lucy whispered.

He would never know that the reason why she had so much trouble getting the words out was because of the terms on which he demanded that she stay. Having lived in a loveless marriage with Ricardo once before, she knew how badly it had affected her. Given the choice, there was no way she was willing to endure that again.

But she didn't have a choice. There was Marco to consider and, just as the first time, the only reason Ricardo was considering this marriage was for his son's sake. Once again, she was going to have to accept the little he was prepared to offer.

And this time he was offering even less than before. At least then they had shared a blazing passion that had warmed their nights and put a spark into their days. Even as she'd grown big with her pregnancy, that fire had been there. It was only when she had given birth to Marco, when Ricardo had his precious legitimate heir, that things had started to change.

If it had stayed that way then she might have been able to bear it. She could at least feel he wanted her in some way. Now it seemed that he didn't want her at all except to create the façade of a respectable marriage.

'I'll stay,' she said again, putting more strength into the words this time. 'My son is worth it.'

She couldn't be in any doubt that he had caught her deliberate echoing of his own words. She had no way of knowing if he understood the very different way she had meant them.

'I will make sure you won't regret it.'

The low-voiced response was so unexpected that it rocked her sense of reality.

'Thank you.'

'*Prego...*'

The twist to his mouth was wry and in the now bright light the fine lines around his eyes, the faint shadows underneath them seemed suddenly more pronounced. He actually looked tired. Was it possible that the last twenty-four hours had knocked him off balance, as they had done to her?

'What made you like this, Ricardo?' The words just wouldn't be held back, even though rational thought warned they might not be wise. 'What made you feel that everything—and everyone—has a price and all you have to do is to pay it to get what you want?'

That twist became more pronounced, turning from sarcasm to out-and-out cynicism. For a moment she thought that he had no intention of answering her but then he shrugged off whatever restraint had been holding him back and started to check off his answers on the fingers of his right hand.

'A grandfather who believed that his daughter was unfit to inherit because she had a child out of wedlock. A father who wanted nothing to do with his bastard son because he did not want to divide his wealth between two children but to leave all to one. Lovers who saw relationships as a passport to wealth and luxury, bought with their bodies in my bed.'

'Then they weren't *lovers*, were they?' Lucy put in, taken

aback by the matter-of-fact tone, the coldly indifferent expression. 'Not really?'

'They called themselves that.'

'Then they lied. Love isn't like that.'

'No? Then tell me—what is it like?'

How did she explain love to a man who didn't even believe that it existed? Who saw relationships only in terms of trade and deals. Of one person giving only because of what they could get in return.

'I…' she began but Ricardo clearly wasn't prepared to wait for her response.

'Are you saying that what we had was this elusive "love"?' Ricardo demanded and the raw edge to his voice caught on something jagged and vulnerable in her heart, twisting brutally. 'Are you saying that what we had was something so very special that nothing could come between us? That we would have each other—hold each other till death us do part?'

'No.' Lucy answered him softly, sadly, because she couldn't say that. Not when it wasn't true, on Ricardo's part at least. 'No, I'm not saying that.'

It was only when she saw the flash of something dark and desolate in his eyes that she had to wonder whether that might have been, after all, what he had been looking for. What he had been trying to find all his life and had never succeeded, with rejection and greed twisting his heart, turning him bitterly cynical, as he was now. The ache inside at the thought was almost unbearable. A terrible sense of what might have been and what they had both lost in the mess they had made of their marriage.

On an impulse, as unexpected to her as it obviously was to Ricardo, suddenly something was pushing her forward, lifting her hands to grasp his arms, pressing her lips against the lean hardness of his cheek.

Immediately everything changed. The scent of his skin was in her nostrils, the taste of him on her tongue, and the rough growth of a day's beard scraped against her cheek, scouring the tender flesh. It was all so wonderfully familiar, so shockingly sensually appealing that her heart kicked once, high up in her chest, then lurched into an uneven rhythm that had her breath escaping on a shaken little gasp.

A gasp that met and blended with the heat and moisture of Ricardo's mouth as he turned and reached for her. Reacting blindly, his eyes half closed, his arms enfolded her as a sharp twist of his body brought him to a position where he was hard against her as his mouth came down on hers in a harsh, possessive kiss. In the space of a single heartbeat it was as if they had both gone up in flames, with the heat and the hunger that built between them taking over their senses, melting their bones and driving them into a burning delirium where nothing existed but each other.

'Lucia…'

Her name was rough and raw against her lips, the taste of his breath as she caught it and blended it with her own inside her mouth was as fiercely intoxicating as any potent spirit, sending her senses spinning out of control. She felt as if the earth were shifting beneath her feet, flinging up her arms to fasten them around Ricardo's neck to steady herself. The action drew his head down to hers to deepen and prolong the kiss in the same moment that it brought their yearning bodies even closer together, clamped tight from breast to hip and thigh, so that she felt the heated evidence of his need, hard and hot against her stomach.

'Rico…'

She couldn't hold back on the once familiar name. The only name she had ever used for him in the intimacy of their bed, in the heat of their lovemaking. She was incapable of getting the full number of syllables out, too greedy for his kisses to separate their mouths for long enough to do so. She didn't even want to snatch a chance to breathe, even though her consciousness threatened to leave her under the sensual assault that ravaged through her senses.

Ricardo's hands were hot on her body, smoothing, caressing, sliding over her hips and cupping the curve of her buttocks, pulling her closer against him. Her breasts were aching and heavy where they crushed against the wall of his chest and the burn of his body heat through the cotton of his shirt combined with the blaze of her own need to make her almost wonder if the night had somehow passed in a flash and the cool light of the moon had been replaced by the scorching heat of the day.

'Yes…' she muttered roughly against his demanding mouth. 'Oh, yes…'

She'd made a terrible mistake and she knew it by the way he froze, his long body going completely still, his mouth wrenching away from her.

'*No!*' he declared roughly, breathing as hard as if he had just run a marathon. '*Maledizione*, no!'

With a violent movement he flung himself away from her, his hands out as if he felt that he needed to hold her at bay, keep her distant from him.

'This is not how it's going to be. We got caught this way once before. It is not going to happen again.'

'Caught?' Lucy questioned, fighting a losing battle with the quaver in her voice.

The look Ricardo turned on her drained all the lingering warmth from her body, shocking her from heat to freezing cold in the space of a single devastated heartbeat.

'Trapped into a marriage that neither of us wanted. That

isn't going to happen again. I will not go there again. Just to look at you, kiss you, might drive me to the edge of madness but I do not have to jump right over the edge. I will not!'

And who was that last declaration directed at? Lucy wondered. At her or at himself? But she didn't have the strength to form the question.

And she didn't have time even to consider an answer because the words had barely died away before Ricardo had raked both hands roughly through his hair, smoothing it back from his face in the same moment that, by some amazingly brutal effort, he brought his breathing and obviously his mind back under total control once more.

'Marissa showed you to the wrong room,' he said, shocking her with the way that he seemed to have taken up the conversation again from the moment that he had first come into the room, as if all the time, all that had happened in between had never existed at all. 'Your suite is down the corridor.'

He clearly expected that she would follow him from the way that he didn't spare a look back but just strode down the corridor to a door that he flung wide open and then stood back to let her in.

With a terrible sense of inevitability, Lucy recognised the room she was in. Ricardo had taken her back to the other bedroom. The one where she had woken—was it really only that morning? The one where he had moved all her clothes, all her belongings, eradicating every trace of her as his wife from his personal space, filing them—and her—away like discarded paperwork.

Finished with. Done.

She had barely stepped inside the room when Ricardo was moving again, turning back towards the room they had just left, dismissing her totally from his thoughts.

'Goodnight, Lucia, *dorme bene*,' he said as the door swung to behind him, cutting him off from her.

Dorme bene. Sleep well.

How could she ever sleep well? How would she manage to sleep at all with all that had happened whirling round and round in her head?

And how was she going to be able to face the first day—and every one after—of this new form of 'marriage' that Ricardo had decreed they would have?

CHAPTER TWELVE

THERE was no way he could sleep. Not now. Not ever, it felt like.

Ricardo's mind was so wired, his whole body burning with the electric aftershock of fierce arousal that he knew there was no way he could lie in a bed and even *think* about sleep. He couldn't even keep still, pacing around his room again and again, wishing to hell that he could get out of here—head for the lake and swim himself into exhaustion. Or work off some of his frustration in the gym, lifting weights and pounding the punchbag until he had managed some form of mental calm.

Calm—hah! That was a joke. A very, very bad joke.

He hadn't had a moment's calm since the day that Lucy Mottram had first walked into his life not quite two years before. He'd been knocked off balance by the wild, heated passion that had rushed them into bed so soon after meeting and he wasn't sure if he'd had a sane thought since then. At least not where she was concerned.

So this time he had decided it would be different. If she came back to the marriage for Marco's sake then he was going to take it so much more slowly. He was going to act with his head and not with the more primitive parts of his anatomy.

It should have made him feel so much more in control, but the truth was that it had had the exact opposite effect. When

Lucy had kissed him he had almost lost it completely. Imposing control for both of them had been a far harder struggle than he had ever imagined. He could fight himself, but fighting Lucy, when she had made it plain how much she wanted him, had been damn near impossible.

He'd even resorted to lying—by implication at least—and letting her think that there had been a stream of women warming his bed in the months they had been apart. Of course there hadn't been. How could there be? He hadn't been able to spare another woman a single glance from the moment that Lucy had walked into his life, and to his total consternation, it had been exactly the same even after she had walked *out* of it again. It seemed that she had taken his libido with her, and memories of how it had been had been all that he'd been left with.

How many times had he scorned, even laughed at the idea when a friend had said that there was only one woman for him? Now he was having to face up to the fact that the damn idea might be true after all. And that Lucy Emiliani, plague of his life, bane of his existence, had turned out to be the one for him. Even when he'd believed that she was only after him for his money, he hadn't cared. Just so long as she stayed in his home, in his bed.

And he still wasn't sure that he'd made the right decision. *Padreterno*—he knew that he hadn't. Not for himself—and not for Lucy, if the look in her eyes when he had walked away from her, leaving her in that other bedroom had been anything to go by.

She hadn't wanted him to leave and he was damn sure that he hadn't wanted to go either. So what the hell was he doing here, fighting with his need for a woman who could affect him like no other female in his life before, when she…?

When she…? What the devil was she doing?

He didn't know—didn't care—because he knew what *he* was doing. There was no going back, no other way out of this. His hand was on the door before he had even realised that he had crossed the room.

In a history of making bad decisions where Lucy Mottram Emiliani was concerned, he was about to make another one. Very possibly the worst he had ever made.

And the truth was that he really didn't give a single damn. He didn't care at all what the consequences might be. He only knew that if he didn't have Lucy in his bed tonight then he would go slowly but surely out of his mind.

He flung the door open, stepped outside.

And stopped dead at the sight of Lucy just emerging from her own room, heading in the direction of his.

Her hair was tumbled about her face and she had made no effort to prepare for bed, still wearing the pink top and skirt that she had worn all day. But her feet were bare, pale and silent on the wooden floor. She froze into stillness in the exact same moment as he did, staring, huge-eyed, straight at him. He only needed one glance at her face, looking deep into her eyes, to know why she was there.

'Rico…' she said and the use of that once intimate, once affectionate form of his name was all he needed to push him right over the edge and into action.

'Lucia…'

He thought that he moved first but they met so fast, so short a way down the silent corridor that she must have come towards him. They collided with a hungry force, each of them with arms coming out to enfold the other, haul them close while their mouths met, clamped, fused in burning need. The strength of the impact slammed them against the wall, Ricardo's body covering Lucy's, his hips cradled in her pelvis, the pressure of her warmth and softness against the hard ache of need he had for her.

His hands were in her hair, twisting in the long golden strands, pulling her face towards him, angling her head just so, so that he could deepen the kiss, plunder her mouth, tangle his tongue with hers. His own breathing was raw in his ears, and hers was every bit as ragged and uneven. Her arms were up around his neck, holding him close, her fingers clenching in the soft short hair at the base of his skull. She was not just being kissed but kissing him back with equal wild enthusiasm.

'Lucia…' he managed in a gasping mutter when the need to snatch in a breath or surrender to unconsciousness forced him to reluctantly release her mouth for a moment. 'I have wanted this—needed this…'

Her soft, uneven little laugh was a sound of acquiescence and agreement, part excitement, part embarrassment. Totally beguiling. But his pulse stilled when she shook her head as it rested against his, her gaze downcast, not looking him in the eyes.

'But you…' The words failed her and she swallowed hard. 'I thought you didn't want a proper marriage.'

Her eyes came up on the last two words, long lashes sweeping the air as blue gaze locked with opaque black. And, with her looking straight into his eyes as she did, what could he say but the truth?

'I lied.'

It was an effort to get the words from a throat that was so raw and thick with need that it seemed it might close up completely but he needed her to hear this. Resting his forehead against hers, looking deep into those clear, beautiful eyes, he tried again.

'*Ho mentito, angelo mio*, I lied.'

I lied…

It was all that Lucy needed to hear. Knowing that Ricardo

had not been able to reject her totally, as she had first believed, sent a rush of heat through her veins, making her pulse throb even more than before. He wanted her as much as she wanted him and, for now, that was enough.

Enough to put an extra urgency into the hungry kiss she pressed on his beautiful mouth. Enough to make her stir against him as the need that throbbed in every nerve became more and more demanding, turning pleasure into something so intense it was close to pain.

Her hands clenched over his strong shoulders, digging into taut muscle in an attempt to get even closer and at the same time keep herself upright as her legs threatened to give way, bones seeming to melt in the blaze of desire that took her by storm. If it wasn't for his powerful support, she felt that she would be sliding down the wall, to land in a molten heap on the floor at his feet.

Ricardo's touch seemed to be everywhere on her body. Hard palms curving over the shape of her buttocks, drawing her even more onto the heat and hardness of his erection, then drifting upwards to tug the pink top free at her waistband, the burn of his fingertips against her bared flesh making her jolt and moan in sharp response.

His lips were on her throat now, making her arch her neck so that his hot mouth could move lower, lingering on the frantic pulse that beat at the base of her neck. And in the same moment he was walking her sideways, along that wall, moving inexorably towards his room where the door had swung open again. He had obviously not stopped to shut it properly in the moment that she had looked up and seen Ricardo in the corridor coming towards her—coming for her.

Her hands were hungry for the feel of him now, needing the warm satin of his skin against them. She pulled his shirt

loose, slipped her hands underneath and felt his hot breath
catch against her throat as he registered her touch. Whirling
away from the support of the wall, he took her with him down
the corridor, blundering from one side to another, slamming
into each wall with such force that she almost feared they
might wake the household, have someone come to find out
what was happening.

But then at last they were in the sanctuary of the room, the
door kicked to behind them. Ricardo swung her up into his
arms, his lips still welded to hers as he carried her across to
the bed, dropping her onto the softly quilted surface and
coming down hard and fast beside her. Her clothes were no
obstacle to his impatient, hungry hands, or his to hers, and
soon everything—shirts, skirt, jeans, underwear—lay in a
tangled heap on the floor, as intimately entwined as their now
naked limbs on the bed.

'I lied,' Ricardo muttered, rough and raw, as first his hands
and then his demanding mouth made contact with her shivering
skin. '*Madre de Dio*, but I lied… How could I not want this…?'

His kiss on her breast made her convulse with a shaken cry,
the pleasure so stunning that it blanked her mind for a
moment, surrendering totally to delight.

'Or this…'

Strong hands smoothed their way down her slender frame,
over the cluster of curls at the core of her body, caressing
fingers sliding knowingly against the tiny focus of her need,
stoking the fire with each touch, building it higher and higher.

It had never been like this before. Not even in the beginning when they had first come together, when the mind-
blowing passion had taken all thought, all sense away from
them, leaving them with only hunger and need. But then everything had been new, a fresh and exciting exploration of

each other's bodies, each other's senses. Now they knew what that passion was like, the intensity of pleasure it could bring, but they had been without it for long, long months, time and distance sharpening hunger, increasing sensation, putting an edge on need.

Then Lucy had been innocent, a touch afraid, unsure of where all this was leading. She had wanted Ricardo so much but at the same time she had been unsure whether he would stay, doubting that she could offer him more than a passing fling and soon he would be on his way again, looking for pastures new. But now, with that deep spoken, heartfelt admission that he had lied about not wanting her still sounding over and over inside her head, she felt newly strong, deeply aware of her feminine power over him. A power revealed in the racing thud of his heart, the streak of burning heat across his hard carved cheekbones, the ragged breathing that he clearly could not pull back under control.

And control was not what she wanted from him. What she wanted was…

'Rico…please…bring us together…make us one.'

'Do you have to ask?' was Ricardo's shaken response.

And then it was as if all his English deserted him, burned up in the heat of the inferno they had built between them and, as he separated her legs, pushing them apart with one long powerful thigh, he resorted to his native Italian to mutter roughly, 'Lucia…*sei bella…quanta ti voglio. Madre de Dio… quanto ti voglio.*'

His ardent litany of need was all that registered in Lucy's mind; the rest of her was totally lost in the sensual assault that was swamping every inch of her body. Her head was spinning, every nerve awake and throbbing, and she was lost and adrift on heated waves of pleasure. Waves that grew higher and

higher with each forceful move of Ricardo's powerful possession, taking her with him further and further until at last they
broke on one final wildest, soaring crest of passion, throwing
her out, his name just a cry on her lips, into the tumbling
oblivion of the most devastating orgasm she had ever known.

It was a long long time before she came back to any sort of
consciousness and then it was only to a drifting, half in and half
out form of reality that held her safe and warm, cushioned in a
hazy oblivion. She was curled up, lax and sated, against the hard
heat of Ricardo's powerful form, enclosed in his arms, hearing
his thudding heart slowly ease into calm under her head, his
breathing even out as, like her, he drifted towards sleep.

'You are mine now,' he muttered, his breath hot against her
neck, his lips pressing kisses on her skin with every word.
'Mine. No one else will ever have you…'

There is no one else…never has been since the day I met you.

The words were there inside Lucy's head, needing to be
said. But, before she could summon up the energy to even
form them, the dark clouds of exhaustion from the day had
rolled over her, taking her mind and her consciousness with
her and dragging her down into the mindlessness of sleep.

Down so deep into the darkness that she should have known.
Should have recognised the mindless, almost comatose state
that always took her over just before the dreams began. The
bleak, lonely dreams filled with terrifying images and sounds.

The dreams that had once driven her out of this house and
away from the man she loved. Away from her child.

Disaster was coming. She could feel it, see it on the
horizon. She had to get away…

'No…'

She was going to have to run all over again. It was much
too dangerous to stay…

…But something was holding her back. Something had hold of her arm, restraining her, and no matter how she tugged…

'Lucy…'

'No…no…'

She couldn't stay. It was too dangerous. Much, much too…

'Lucia, *tesoro*… Listen to me…I'm here…*angelo mio*…'

Suddenly there was a faint light in her eyes. And in that faint light a darker shape. A strength and solidity that stood out from the shadows, making her blink in shock and confusion.

'Lucia…' the voice said softly again.

Warm arms came round her, holding her softly, comforting, protecting, not restraining. Where was she? Who was with her?

What the devil was happening here? Ricardo asked himself as he tried to keep his hold on Lucy careful and soft. Never wake a sleepwalker, everyone said. But then everyone had not been confronted by the sight of their wife heading for the stairs, totally naked and with her eyes so blank that it was obvious she wasn't seeing anything in reality.

He'd been woken by her restlessness. The tossing and turning in her sleep that had made it plain that, whatever was happening in her dreams, it was far from pleasant. The dawn had just been breaking when she had first actually sat up, throwing back the bedclothes and swinging her feet to the ground.

'What is it? Where are you going?' he'd asked but she hadn't replied. Instead she'd ignored him completely, standing up and heading for the door. In the end, realising that she was walking in her sleep, he had been left with no choice but to follow her, snatching up the robe that lay across the bed as he went, knowing she was going to need that, whatever happened.

He'd followed her down the corridor, stunned to see she found her way without any hesitation even though her eyes were wide and unfocused, staring straight at nothing.

But when she'd headed for the top of the stairs, that had been a different matter. In spite of everything he'd heard, he couldn't just stand back and watch. He 'd taken her hand very gently, holding her back without a word. But now she had stopped and had turned away from the danger. She was looking at him—looking but not seeing with those wide unfocused eyes.

'Where are you going, *cara*?' he asked again.

'I…I was looking for Marco. My baby.'

'He's fine…' Ricardo began reassuringly but Lucy just talked across him as if he hadn't spoken, her voice rising sharply in evident distress.

'I have to find him. But I mustn't touch him—I mustn't *harm* him!'

Harm? The word sounded shocking, appalling in Ricardo's thoughts. How could she even think that she might harm the baby? Anyone who had ever seen her with him would know that that was an impossibility. That was why he had been so shocked when she had run out on their child. His thoughts went back to the way that Lucy has described her illness earlier that day. She had explained, but it seemed that she hadn't told him everything that had happened. Hadn't told him everything she had been through.

'You won't harm Marco, *tesoro*. He's quite safe.'

He kept his voice quiet, steady, and she seemed to respond to it. The wide-eyed stare was just a little less wild and her slender body perhaps not quite so tense. She was shivering though, whether from nerves or the cool of the pre-dawn, he didn't know, but he slipped the robe around her as gently as he could and knew an almost shocking sense of satisfaction to see her respond and huddle herself into it, drawing it closer round her.

'I have to keep Marco safe,' she said again and he was relieved to hear that some of the frantic note had left her voice too.

'He's safe. I promise you he is. He's completely safe.'

And then she said the words that stunned him completely, hitting him like a punch in the gut so that he almost doubled up from it.

'He will be,' she said. 'He'll be safe when I'm gone.'

Just what could he say to answer that? There was nothing. He could think of nothing and, besides, you couldn't argue or even discuss something with a woman who, for all she was walking and talking, was still actually sound asleep.

'He'll be fine,' he managed, knowing he had to say something. 'And so will you. You'll see him in the morning. But you should get some sleep first—come back to bed.'

To his relief, she didn't resist, letting him lead her carefully away from the danger of the wide, curving staircase, back down the corridor. She followed him, placid as an exhausted child, only slowing, then resisting as they neared his bedroom door.

'Not this way…my husband…Ricardo…mustn't know. He'll hate me.'

Hate?

Lucy was obviously fading now and, needing to make sure she didn't collapse, on he hastily led her past the half-closed door and took her to her own room instead. Once inside she seemed to relax, losing all the tension that gripped her and slumping back against the wall in obvious exhaustion. Swinging her up into his arms, Ricardo carried her to the bed and laid her on it carefully, pulling the covers up around her. Lucy sighed softly, already drifting away back into sleep.

'Stay…' she whispered, tightening the fingers that were still entwined with his. 'Stay.'

'Of course.'

As he slid in beside her she turned, snuggling closer, resting her head against his shoulder, the fine strands of her hair lying like silk against his chest. Ricardo folded his arms around her, holding her so that he felt her slim body relax into sleep, the nightmare or whatever it had been forgotten in the oblivion of unconsciousness.

But he could not forget. And as she slept so deeply beside him he lay wide awake, staring with unseeing eyes up at the ceiling, remembering and thinking.

And later, when he was sure that he would not disturb her, he slipped from the bed, moving as silently as he could, heading out of the room and down the long corridor towards his office.

CHAPTER THIRTEEN

IT WAS the sense of something being wrong that dragged Lucy from her sleep the next morning. A feeling that something had changed forcing her into unwilling wakefulness, making her stir in the comfort of the bed.

And that was when a feeling of loss slid into her mind so that she frowned uncertainly, still keeping her eyes closed.

Something wasn't right here. The bed felt too big, too empty. She had fallen asleep feeling safe, secure for the first time in months, had slept soundly, dreamlessly, but now it felt as if something was missing.

She opened her eyes slowly, slowly, reluctantly. She felt as if she had been dragged from the depths of a dark pit, surfacing unwillingly into the living world. It almost seemed as if she had a hangover, except that she knew she hadn't had a single drink the night before.

And then memory returned. Hazy images of being out of bed, in the corridor outside surfacing in her mind. She knew what this feeling meant. It was one that she had experienced so often before, in the darkest days of her illness. When the staff at the hospital would tell her the next morning what had happened in the night.

She had been sleepwalking again.

But why? In the past such episodes had been linked to stress. To the fears and miseries she'd endured after leaving the villa. She had thought—had hoped that they were over for good. But it seemed that she'd been wrong. The realisation made her turn her face into the pillow, groaning aloud at the thought.

'*Buon giorno*, Lucia.'

The voice came from near the window, bringing her eyes open in a rush to stare straight into Ricardo's watchful face as other memories flooded her thoughts, making them reel.

That final confrontation; the cold-blooded declaration he had made that she should act as his wife and yet not *be* his wife, that was a source enough for the stress that had triggered the attack. And not just that…

Heat ran through every inch of her body as she recalled that the evening had not ended with Ricardo's declaration. She had tried to stay in her room, determined, for now, to work with what she had. At least Ricardo had agreed to let her stay. At least she could be a mother to Marco. Just forty-eight hours before, she would have settled for that and been thankful for it. But here, now, she knew there was no way she could do so.

So she had left her room, going back to talk to Ricardo…

And she had met him in the corridor, coming to find her.

As she struggled to sit up, the realisation that she wore a black towelling robe, gaping at the front, brought other memories flooding back in a rush. Memories that made her skin burn with remembered heat. The molten passion that had brought them together had seared her right to her soul, leaving her stunned and shattered, not knowing what this meant for the future of their relationship, if they had one. It was no wonder that her old fears had resurfaced, driving her out of her bed and into wandering the house while still asleep.

And there had been one other thing, one final straw that

had truly broken her back, emotionally at least. It had been there, in her mind, as she fell asleep and it had obviously filled her thoughts, disturbed her dreams.

There is no one else…never has been since the day I met you.

In the twilight place between waking and sleeping, her mind had broken free of the restraints she had tried to impose on it. In that half-and-half world, she had been unable to pretend to herself any more, as the need, the yearning—the love she still felt had forced its way into her unshielded mind.

She might have told herself that she was staying for Marco. She might declare that fact to Ricardo's face and assure him that the baby was what she wanted. She might try to believe it, need to believe it was the truth for her own emotional safety. But the reality was very far from that.

She wanted to stay *to be with Ricardo*. No matter what conditions he imposed on her living on the island; no matter what role he expected her to play, she would take the little he offered with both hands, grab it and hold it for as long as he let her, so long as it meant that she could be close to the man that she loved.

'G-good morning,' she managed, wondering as she spoke whether the words were really appropriate. The atmosphere in the room felt thick and clouded, as if a fog were filling up her lungs, choking her, making it difficult to breathe. She had the most unnerving feeling that the Ricardo she was facing this morning was a man she had never met before in her life.

He was sitting in a chair near the window, his long body apparently relaxed, long legs stretched out in front of him, crossed at the ankle. But his face denied the appearance of relaxation, with every muscle looking tight and drawn in a way that hardened his jaw, thinned his beautiful mouth and made his eyes into piercing lasers that subjected her face to such scrutiny that she almost felt as if they might scour off a layer or more of skin.

In contrast to her rumpled and still half-awake state, Ricardo must have been up and out of the bed for some time. He had obviously showered and shaved; his black hair was still slick with moisture and just beginning to dry in the warmth of the day. And he was fully dressed in tailored shirt and trousers, the formal style of his clothes, together with their sombre, all black colouring combining to create an impression that was cold and remote as well as ominously dangerous and controlled.

'I made some coffee,' was his surprisingly casual comment, a wave of his hand indicating the tray that stood on a table by his chair. 'Would you like some?'

'OK. Yes, please.'

If her voice shook slightly it was because of the confusion in her mind. However she had seen this 'morning after the night before' working out, it was not like this.

She had hoped—dreamed—that she might wake up in Ricardo's arms. That, safe and warm—and close—they might have a chance to start the new day in a very different way from how they had yesterday. A chance to start again. What she had feared, the fears growing stronger when she had sensed that the bed beside her was empty and Ricardo had got up, was that he had decided that their night together had been a terrible mistake and that he would decree they must go back to the no sex non-marriage he had declared they must have.

Instead, what she had was a near exact repeat of waking up the previous day. As if nothing had changed when in fact everything had.

Deciding she would feel better if she could face him on more equal terms, she scrambled out of bed while Ricardo was pouring coffee and pulled on the robe that lay over the end of the bed, knotting the tie belt and yanking it tight around her waist. The sleeves hung loosely over her hands, the length of it falling almost to her ankles, and she could probably have wrapped the front a couple of times around herself and still have plenty to spare. Only now did she belatedly realise that the reason it was so big and ill fitting was because it was actually Ricardo's robe and so more than several sizes too big for her.

That thought made her distinctly nervous, as it pushed her to recall yet more of the night before. It was the touch and the feel of the towelling robe that brought it back, the evocative scent of Ricardo's skin on the soft material. In the night when she had been sleepwalking, someone had put that robe around her and...

Her throat was so tight that it hurt as she recalled how he had called her *tesoro, angelo mio*, the soft voice full of concern. A voice so very different from the one he had used since she had woken this morning.

So what had happened in the night? What had she done? What had she said? The questions sent a sensation like the slither of something nasty and very cold down her spine so that when Ricardo brought the coffee over to her she reached for it with enthusiasm, hoping it would warm her chilled body, ease the tension in her throat.

'Thank you.'

She was relieved to find that this time her voice was actually quite strong and even. At least the way she felt inside was hidden from him for now. But how long that would last when he stood so close, the clean scent of his fresh-from-the-shower skin reaching out to enclose her, the softness of his newly drying hair making her fingers itch to touch, she didn't know. Just to look at his mouth was to recall how it had felt on her skin, the sinful pleasures it had awoken, the hunger she hadn't been able to control.

Edging carefully back, she came up against the bed and perched awkwardly on the side, struggling with the drowning looseness of the robe. A quick sip of the coffee brought some much needed warmth into her veins.

'About last night...' she began, edgy and unsure but knowing that she couldn't leave the topic hanging between them, with both of them avoiding it.

'Last night was last night,' Ricardo answered calmly, his carved features showing no response. 'And what happened then is one thing. Today is a whole new day—and things have changed.'

'Changed how?' Lucy questioned edgily, unease making her shift uncomfortably from one foot to another on the soft cream coloured carpet. 'And where do we go from here?'

'That's what I want to find out.'

Ricardo didn't return to his chair, instead he paced around the room, back and forth.

'And the only way forward is for you to tell me the real truth.'

That made Lucy's heart clench, her throat tightening so that she almost choked on her coffee.

'I have been telling you the truth!'

'Not the whole truth. At least not where your illness was concerned.'

And then Lucy knew where he was going with this. In spite of the weight and warmth of the robe, her skin felt suddenly chilled and clammy, so that she had to fight to control a shiver of real apprehension.

How had she revealed things last night? What had she told him of the darkest days of her illness, the terrible fears and thoughts that had assailed her? And how was that going to affect their relationship from now on? The future that she had thought they would have together?

'Ricardo…' she began stumblingly but he held up a hand to silence her.

'No—let me.'

Prowling over to the window again, he sat down on the wide window seat, staring out for a moment at where the waters of the lake sparkled in the sunlight, before he turned back to her. His expression was totally blanked off, eyes dark and hooded.

'You told me you were ill. You didn't tell how ill. You said you had a breakdown.'

'Post-natal depression.' Lucy's voice was low and unsteady.

'But it wasn't just that, was it? You weren't just depressed—you were…'

With a rough, almost angry movement he raked both his hands through his hair, shaking his head roughly as he did so.

'Last night you went sleepwalking—out of the room, along the corridor. You said you were looking for Marco.'

As Lucy drew in a sharp, uneasy breath his dark eyes flashed to her face and locked with her own worried gaze.

'You were lost. Frightened. You thought you'd lost him. But you were also scared of finding him—scared that you might harm him.'

'That was the way I felt sometimes. I felt…separate from him—I couldn't bond with him.'

And with those words—the words she had struggled with most—finally said, suddenly it was as if the wall in her mind had come down and the words were just tumbling out, faster and faster, falling over each other in the need to have them said.

'There were times when I couldn't even believe that Marco

was mine—ours. I thought that I was going mad—or that the world I lived in was crazy. I dreamed that I'd harmed him—maybe even killed him and so I'd go into his nursery to check if he was all right. But if he woke then he just cried and cried until the nanny came and only then would he stop. The nanny could stop him crying but I couldn't. I felt that he hated me—that I wasn't really his mother and he sensed that.'

'Post-natal psychosis,' Ricardo said when at last she came to a halt. 'Not just post-natal depression but the psychosis I looked it up on the Internet,' he added at her start of surprise. 'I've been reading all damn night. Why the hell didn't you tell someone?'

Carefully Lucy put down her cup on the bedside table so that the way her hands were shaking wouldn't mean that she spilled the rapidly cooling coffee all over the floor. She couldn't drink it anyway. Her stomach was tying itself in knots and she felt sick. Ricardo had accepted the depression but this was something else entirely. This was something that affected his precious son.

'I didn't know what was happening to me and I was afraid to tell anyone. I was scared—terrified.'

'Terrified of what?' Ricardo demanded harshly.

'Of you.'

Her low-voiced response might actually have been a blow aimed at him. She saw his long body jerk just once in response to it.

'Terrified that you would throw me out. That you wouldn't want me when you had what you wanted—Marco. Specially not when you thought that I was a danger to him—and at the time I was convinced that I would harm him. Perhaps I already had.'

'And so you left.'

Ricardo got slowly to his feet once more, resuming that restless pacing up and down as if he felt imprisoned and was hunting for a way out—any way out.

'I couldn't see any other way to go. I thought I'd feel better if I just got away. But I didn't feel any better—the truth was that I felt a whole lot worse. And that was when I knew I needed help.'

'And you turned to a doctor.'

It was impossible to interpret the meaning in Ricardo's comment. She couldn't read anything from the flat, inflexionless words.

'Who else was there for me to turn to? You know my mother and I have never been able to talk—not properly. And there wasn't anyone else. Certainly not you. I could never have gone to you. We didn't have that sort of marriage. Not any sort of real marriage. Not then—not now.'

'You're damn right not now!'

Even as the words were flung in her face, Ricardo was turning on his heel and heading for the door. Lucy could only stare after him in blank bemusement, not knowing what had happened or what was going through his head.

'Ricardo…'

Her shaken use of his name brought him to an abrupt halt. Just for a moment he paused, then he turned back very slowly. For a long drawn-out moment he simply stared at her, eyes narrowed, his mouth clamped into a thin hard line. Then at last he drew in a deep, uneven breath.

'What you're saying,' he said at last and the sound of the ruthless control he was imposing on his voice made a horrible sensation like the march of tiny, icy footprints move slowly up and down Lucy's spine. 'What you're saying is that it wasn't the illness—the post-natal depression—that drove you away from here. It wasn't anything that was wrong with you—it was everything that was wrong with us. We should never have married and that was what was at the root of things all along.'

His words dropped into a silence that Lucy had no idea how to fill. How could she when the only words that she could say were *yes* and *you're right*? That was exactly where the problem lay and hearing it stated in such blunt, unequivocal terms stripped all the strength to respond from her, paralysing her voice so that she could only nod in silent, desperate agreement.

'The only thing I do not understand,' Ricardo went on, still in that terrible flat, emotionless voice, 'is why the devil you ever came back. Once you had got away, why not stay away—as far away as possible?'

And there was only one answer to that.

'You know why,' Lucy managed, her voice just a thin thread of sound. 'Marco.'

'Marco,' Ricardo echoed heavily, nodding slowly in impassive agreement. 'Of course.'

'You do see…'

'Of course I see.' He almost smiled but it was a terrible, bleak smile, one that had no light in it whatsoever. 'What else could you do? For Marco. You were quite right about that—and right about our marriage too. That was the worst possible mistake, right from the start. It was never going to work. It is never going to work.'

He'd turned again, was wrenching the door wide open with a violence that almost tore it from its hinges.

'It ends now,' he tossed over his shoulder, not looking back, striding determinedly away from her as if he couldn't wait to put distance between them. 'I'm ending it now. It's best we forget the whole marriage idea and go our separate ways, I'll get my solicitor onto it right away.'

CHAPTER FOURTEEN

SOMEHOW Lucy managed to force herself to get dressed.

It was a struggle to make herself take off Ricardo's robe and drape it over a chair, when she was longing to hold onto it, to huddle inside it, inhale the lingering traces of his personal scent that clung to the fabric in a way she clearly could no longer do with the man who owned it.

But she needed to feel covered, protected—armoured against whatever might come next. She had no idea when Ricardo might come back and what he had planned if he did, but she had to be ready. She found a pair of jeans and a T-shirt amongst the clothes in the wardrobe and pulled them on, grimacing at the way that the jeans hung off her. Had she really lost that much weight while she'd been ill?

The knock at the door came just as she was fastening a belt around her waist to hold them up. Had Ricardo come back already? And, if he had, then was that good news or bad? Had he changed his mind…?

The thoughts died in her head as she opened the door to find one of the maids standing outside.

Of course. Ricardo would never have knocked. He would have just marched straight in without waiting to be asked.

'Yes?' she asked uncertainly, the apprehension that gripped

her growing as the young woman poured out a string of rapid Italian. Lucy couldn't completely understand, but got the gist of something that sounded like 'Pack now? Are you ready for me to pack all your clothes?' And the way that the maid indicated a suitcase she had brought with her seemed to confirm that that was what she meant.

'I don't understand... Why would you want to pack for me?'

The answer was another tirade of Italian, foremost of which—and totally without needing any translation—was the constantly repeated 'Signor Emiliani'.

Signor Emiliani said this... Signor Emiliani did that... Signor Emiliani had instructed her to pack, ready for the Signora to leave.

Oh, *had* he?

Lucy didn't stop to think, only reacted. She was out of the door in a second, rushing down the corridor before she had time to think. He was throwing her out. After he'd had what he wanted, he was getting rid of her. So much for all his promises to let her stay.

She didn't know if what she was feeling was agonising pain, sheer blind fury or a dangerously volatile and potentially lethal combination of both. She only knew that she was going to find him and have this out with him. She couldn't settle until she did.

He was no longer in his bedroom, but she had a strong suspicion of just where she might find him. If he was busy organising things and issuing orders left, right and centre, then there was one place he was likely to be.

She was right. When she marched straight into his office—not allowing herself to pause at the doorway for fear she might lose all her courage and back down, maybe even run away—it was to find Ricardo sitting at his desk, a litter of papers spread out before him, his dark head bent over something he was writing.

'I said come back in half an hour!' he snapped, not looking up and obviously mistaking her for someone else.

'Oh, really?' Lucy questioned cynically. 'I got the impression that I was to go away and not come back at all—ever—wasn't that what you said?'

Ricardo's head came up fast in astonishment, and the look she caught in his dark eyes shocked and disturbed her. For just a moment he looked like a completely different man.

She couldn't put a name to what she had seen and it didn't stay around long enough for her to take it further. One swift blink and it was gone and in its place was cold, hard rejection.

'Lucia! I sent someone to…'

'I know you sent someone to pack for me—to make sure I got out of your house as quickly as possible—but I have news for you. I'm not going.'

Deliberately she folded her arms across her chest, chin lifting defiantly. She even planted her feet wide apart on the gold and blue rug before the desk, challenging him to come and move her if he dared.

'And don't call me Lucia.'

She wasn't going to let him know how much it hurt to hear his own personal version of her name on his lips, spoken in that seductive accent. It had once meant so much to her. But that had been when she had believed they had a relationship.

'My name is Lucy.'

Ricardo's mouth twisted in a wry smile.

'I know,' he said and there was almost a note of amusement in his tone. 'Lucy is what I just wrote here. Lucy Emiliani, soon to be Lucy Mottram again.'

He tapped his pen down on the topmost piece of paper on

his desk, making Lucy crane forward to read. She gasped as she realised that it was a cheque—obviously a replacement for the one he had written before, which she had torn to shreds and scattered to the winds. A cheque for the same impossibly huge amount of money that he had offered her then.

'I told you I didn't want that. As I recall, I ripped up one cheque already—'

'That was when I thought I wanted you to stay.'

If he'd flung the pen right at her heart he couldn't have made a deadlier hit, and Lucy could only be glad that she already had her arms folded around herself because they went some way towards holding her together when she felt she was falling apart.

'And now?'

The look Ricardo turned on her told its own story. *What do you think?* was stamped onto those hard, unyielding features.

'Is this your answer to everything, Ricardo? Throw money at it until it goes away? So you think you can pay me to leave, do you?'

'It's something I can do for you. The only thing. Pay to support you when you do leave,' Ricardo corrected but Lucy was too far gone to recognise exactly what the difference was in what he said.

'Well, you can think again. I'm not leaving. Not now—not ever—not when you think you can break your promise and get away with it.'

'Promise?' Ricardo pounced on the word as if she had said something exceptional and his dark brows snapped together in a quick hard frown. 'Break what promise?'

That had Lucy unfolding her arms and flinging them in the air in total exasperation.

'What promise? Oh, come on, Ricardo! You know perfectly well! You promised me that I would see my baby—see Marco again—'

'And you will.'

'What—to say goodbye?' Lucy choked on the words, finding them almost impossible to get out through the thickness of tears clogging up her throat. Tears she was determined that Ricardo was not going to see her shed. 'You'll allow me that? Well, thank you so very much! How cruel can you be!'

'Not to say goodbye.' Ricardo pushed back his chair roughly, getting to his feet and raking both hands roughly through his hair in a gesture of frustration. 'You'll see him when you collect him ready for the journey.'

She had to be imagining things, Lucy told herself. The stress had finally got to her and she was hearing things that there was no way that Ricardo could ever have said.

'What journey? I don't understand,' she stammered. 'Where is he going?'

'Wherever you're going.'

Then, when she still gaped at him, too bemused to take anything in, he shook his head with a strange mixture of resignation and impatience.

'Wherever you're going, then Marco is going with you. He's leaving with you. You're both going together.'

'He…you are joking. You have to be.'

'No joke. Why would I joke about this?'

Ricardo's eyes met hers with a burning intensity that left her no room for doubt that he meant exactly what he said.

'When you leave, Marco is going with you. I won't contest your custody. All that I ask is that you allow me access as often as possible.'

'Of course I…' Lucy couldn't complete the sentence but broke off in total confusion. This couldn't be happening. You don't need to do this. You have custody of Marco and you can keep him here. Why are you doing this?'

'If I keep Marco here, then you will never leave,' Ricardo told her starkly. In a series of impossible things that he'd said since she had come into the room, that was the most unbelievable of all.

'You're so determined to get rid of me that you'll give your son away to achieve it?'

'You are his mother. I know you will love him and care for him. I also know it cannot be any other way.' Ricardo's voice seemed to have developed a raw and disturbing edge. He sounded as if his words were coming unravelled at the edges, disintegrating as he spoke them. 'I know that you won't leave without him. So how can I set you free unless I do this?'

Now Lucy knew that she was hearing things. Had he really said *set you free*?

'How can you set me free—and, more importantly, why?'

'Oh, Lucy…'

The deliberate effort he made to use the English form of her name caught on something raw and painful deep in Lucy's heart.

'Isn't it obvious? I'm letting you out of this marriage. That's what you want, isn't it? I trapped you into a marriage you didn't want once before. I'll not do so again.'

A marriage *you* didn't want. Was it possible that Ricardo was saying that *he* had wanted it? No—no way! Hadn't he always emphasised that he had never wanted marriage? That he was only marrying her because of the baby.

But hadn't she been the one to drive that home too? Saying she would marry him for the baby—and only for the baby. Because it was what she'd thought he'd wanted.

'You didn't trap me,' Lucy said carefully. She was manoeuvring blind here, feeling her way inch, by wary inch and if she put a foot wrong then she might fall flat on her face from a very great height. 'If anything, I trapped myself by being so stupid—so naïve about the contraception thing. But when you asked me, I went into our marriage of my own free will. I didn't have to marry you. But it was…I knew it was what you wanted. For Marco.'

'For Marco at the beginning, perhaps, but later…'

'Are you saying…?'

Oh, dear heaven, no! She wasn't brave enough to go so far so fast. Not without something from him that would give her room to hope. Carefully, nervously, she took a couple of steps forward towards where Ricardo now stood by the side of the desk. This close she could see the faintly bruised shadows under his eyes, the fine lines of strain that feathered out from the corners, and had to wonder just what stress had put them there.

'We could have made a better job of it,' she began but Ricardo had launched into speech at the same time.

'If you hadn't felt trapped you would never have left— would never have gone to some doctor hundreds of miles away. Someone you'd never seen before.'

It seemed to Lucy as if the atmosphere in the room had totally changed again, so that she felt as if the earth were shifting under her feet, dangerously rocking her sense of reality.

'But I needed help.'

'You could have had help. You did have help.'

'I did?'

That was too much to take in. Lucy's hand went to her head to try and ease the intolerable pressure there as she fought to absorb what was happening.

Had she got this so terribly wrong?

'You could have come to me—you *should* have come to me. If we had had any sort of a marriage, if I had been any sort of a husband, I would have been there for you. I was there for you. All you had to do was ask.' Fire blazed in Ricardo's eyes, burning away the dazed look that she now realised had been there before. 'Why did you not come to me? Did you not trust me?'

That wasn't anger in his voice. It was pain—a real, deep, soul-destroying pain. She had *hurt* him. Not just by running out on their marriage, on Marco, but, earlier than that, worse than that, by not trusting him, not telling him that she needed help and giving him the chance to offer it.

'We didn't have that sort of a marriage. I knew that what mattered most to you was your child. I knew you'd fight anything, destroy anything that threatened his safety.'

'Did you truly think that I would destroy you?'

The raw hoarseness of his voice gave her the answer to that question and the painful sting of her conscience had her reaching out, catching his hands and holding them tightly. He let his fingers lie in hers, not responding, but at least he didn't pull away.

'I was afraid,' Lucy managed, her own voice not much stronger than his, but it had to work. She had to make him believe what she was saying. 'Afraid that you'd throw me out.'

'And so you pre-empted my actions—the actions you thought I'd take. You didn't wait around for me to throw you out. You went yourself.'

'I thought that was my only way out. I didn't know how to talk to you. You were always so busy. And we hadn't made love for weeks.'

'You were the one who moved into another room. And I let you go because I thought that you were tired—exhausted from having the baby.'

'I was…' Lucy put in but Ricardo continued as if she hadn't spoken.

'You went away for days and would never say where you'd been.'

Lucy felt tears burn at the back of her eyes as she recalled the flippant, careless way she had dismissed his questions, the way she had felt that he was criticising her, trying to control her life.

'The truth was that I didn't know where I'd been—I was living in a haze most of the time. I just went out, went over to the mainland and walked…'

'I should have gone with you—followed you. I should have tried harder. I knew that something was wrong but I was too damn blind to see what it was. When I met you I wanted you so badly—you seemed so fresh and so innocent. So different from any woman I'd known before.'

But then she had turned him down at that first meeting. Only to fall into his arms—into his bed—when she had met the real Ricardo Emiliani a few days later.

'I always regretted saying no to you that first time. You don't know how much I regretted it—wished for a second chance. When I got that second chance I knew I had to grab at it with both hands—not risk letting it escape me again. I didn't even stop to think…'

Something was different, though, she realised. He was actually holding her hands now, having twisted his own round in her grip until his fingers were the ones curled around hers. It was a little thing but it was progress.

'I *wanted* you to be different. I was starting to believe that you could be different. But when the spending started—it was the pattern I'd seen before. I was so disappointed. So angry that it blinded me to any other possible reason for your behaviour.'

'I actually thought that the things I bought would make me feel better,' Lucy admitted. 'That this dress or that top would be the one that would restore my self-esteem, make me look good again. But then, when I got it home, it wasn't the magic I needed. And…' Her voice caught on the words, a small gasping sob escaping from the rawness of her throat. 'I wanted you to see me again—really see me. I wanted you to think that I was beautiful…'

That got a reaction from him. His head came up sharply, black eyes blazing into blue.

'But you were so beautiful—more beautiful then than at any time since I'd met you.' Ricardo freed one hand, lifting it and smoothing it through her hair before cradling her cheek in his palm. 'Except for now,' he murmured. 'From the moment I saw you on the beach, I knew I was lost. I wasn't prepared to admit it to myself at the time, but I knew that I had to have you back in my life. No matter what it took.'

'Even to the extent of declaring that you didn't want a proper marriage?' Lucy risked, and a tiny bubble of joy danced in her throat when she heard his faint laughter in response.

'And implying that I had had other women since you left— that was another lie too,' Ricardo acknowledged. 'Not one of my better decisions, I admit. But I was determined to take things steady this time, work with my head, not the passion I feel for you. The passion that scrambles my thoughts, makes me act irrationally—crazily. This time I wanted to keep a clear head.' His mouth twisted wryly. 'I didn't manage to last very long.'

'Nor did I,' Lucy reminded him. 'It was what we both wanted.'

'But it was too soon—too fast—just like the first time. That was when we made the mistake. This time I wanted us to have space to get to know each other. Time to…'

Lucy's breath caught in her throat. *Time to…* Had he been about to say *time to learn to love each other*? But Ricardo didn't complete the sentence.

'If you had known me better when Marco was born, then you might have been able to talk to me. You should have been able to talk to me but I failed you. Do you know what it did to me when you said that you had been afraid to talk—afraid of me?'

There was no need for words to describe what he'd felt. It was there in the sheen on his eyes, the tremor of pain in his voice, the way his hands tightened around hers. She could be in no doubt as to what he'd gone through, hearing those words.

'I felt that I'd lost you—that there was no way back from that. That was when I decided I had to let you go.'

'I tried…' Lucy broke off sharply, her breath catching in her throat as she felt Ricardo's strong arms come round her. He drew her close, held her against his side. And it was not a sexual approach, not at heart, but a gesture of comfort and support, warm and gentle.

She would almost dare to say it was a gesture of love.

'I was wrong to make you feel that,' he admitted deeply. 'At the time you didn't seem to need me. I know now that you needed me more than ever before in your life, but I was too blind to see that. I'll never forgive myself…'

He broke off as Lucy's hand came over his mouth to still the words.

'But you must! You must forgive yourself. If I can forgive you—and myself—for what happened then, you can. You must!'

Her heart leapt as she felt the pressure of his kiss, soft and warm against her fingers. Looking up into those deep, dark eyes, she drew on all her courage to ask the most important question. She felt she knew that the answer she wanted was there, but she needed to hear it, to have him say it.

'Ricardo, you said that you wanted to set me free. Why did…?'

'Because I can't keep you here in a marriage you don't

want. It would be like caging a beautiful bird and I can't do that to the woman I love. If you don't want our marriage then I want you to be happy. I want you to be free—free to go out into the world and find someone you can love, as I love you. As I will love you for the rest of my life.'

…someone you can love, as I love you. As I will love you for the rest of my life.

What more could she ask for? What more did she need? Everything she had dreamed of, longed for, was in those two sentences. Words that would sustain her for as long as she lived.

'I don't think I can,' she said slowly and saw his dark head go back, his eyes widening in shock as he looked down into her intent face. 'I don't think I can ever be free—that I can ever *want* to be free. I can't go out into the world and be happy because I can't leave our marriage—it would kill me to do so. And I can't find someone to love—because I've already found him… He's here…'

Slowly, carefully, she lifted her hands and rested them on either side of his handsome face, cupping it between both of her palms, and she met his searching gaze with a whole new confidence.

'You're here. And you're the man—the only man—I want. I love you, Ricardo. Love you with all my heart. I want nothing more than to start again. To have a future with you. To be married to you. A real marriage this time. A marriage of two hearts.'

'A marriage of love,' Ricardo murmured as he bent his head to take her lips in a long, loving caress. 'I couldn't ask for anything more.'

His kiss made her senses swim, set her heart racing. And the way that his strong arms held her close, tight up against the heated power of his hard body, left her in no doubt that

Ricardo too was as forcefully affected as she was. And that left her with one more thing she needed to say.

'Ricardo,' she whispered against his lips, taking tiny gentle kisses from them with each word. 'In this marriage of love that we'll have—at some time in the future I'd love a brother or sister for Marco. But I'm scared—terrified it might happen again.'

Ricardo's arms tightened around her and feeling his strength seeming to pour into her she already felt her fears start to ebb away before its force.

'If it does, then this time I'll be there at your side, night and day, however long it takes,' Ricardo assured her, his voice deep and husky with love. 'I'll be with you—give you whatever support, whatever help you need. I promise.'

His kiss was long and slow, an affirmation of love that would be there for her no matter what happened. And Lucy felt her heart lift in response to it, the certainty that they could handle this if it came.

'And this time I won't be afraid to ask for it,' she murmured, returning his kiss, deepening it. Putting all her heart and her soul into it.

'This time we'll do it together,' Ricardo said and she knew that it was a promise, not just for now but for the whole of their future.

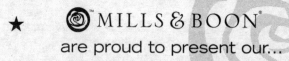

millsandboon.co.uk Community

Join Us!

The Community is the perfect place to meet and chat to kindred spirits who love books and reading as much as you do, but it's also the place to:

- Get the inside scoop from authors about their latest books
- Learn how to write a romance book with advice from our editors
- Help us to continue publishing the best in women's fiction
- Share your thoughts on the books we publish
- Befriend other users

Forums: Interact with each other as well as authors, editors and a whole host of other users worldwide.

Blogs: Every registered community member has their own blog to tell the world what they're up to and what's on their mind.

Book Challenge: We're aiming to read 5,000 books and have joined forces with The Reading Agency in our inaugural Book Challenge.

Profile Page: Showcase yourself and keep a record of your recent community activity.

Social Networking: We've added buttons at the end of every post to share via digg, Facebook, Google, Yahoo, technorati and de.licio.us.

www.millsandboon.co.uk

SAVE OVER £60

Free L'Occitane Gift Set worth OVER £10

As you enjoy reading Mills & Boon® Modern™
titles we are offering you the chance to
sign up for 12 months and SAVE £61.25 –
that's a fantastic 40% OFF.

If you prefer, you can sign up for 6 months and
SAVE £19.14 – that's still an impressive 25% OFF.

When you sign up you will receive 4 BRAND-NEW Modern
titles a month priced at just £1.91 each if you opt for a 12-
month subscription or £2.39 each if you opt for 6 months.
The full price of each book would normally cost you £3.19.

*PLUS, to say thank you, we will send you a
FREE L'Occitane Gift Set worth over £10*.*

You will also receive many more great benefits, including:
- **FREE home delivery**
- **EXCLUSIVE Mills & Boon® Book Club™ offers**
- **FREE monthly newsletter**
- **Titles available before they're in the shops**

Subscribe securely online today and SAVE up to 40% @ www.millsandboon.co.uk

*Gift set has an RRP of £10.50 and includes Verbena Shower Gel 75ml and Soap 110g.